THE GOOD GUY CHALLENGE

LAUREN BLAKELY

COPYRIGHT

Copyright © 2022 by Lauren Blakely
LaurenBlakely.com
Cover Design by © Qamber Designs & Media

authorized, associated with, or sponsored by the trademark owners. This is a work of fiction. Names, characters, business, events and incidents are the products of the author's imagination. Any resemblance to actual persons, living or dead, or actual events is purely coincidental.

ABOUT THE GOOD GUY CHALLENGE

Fake real dating the one who got away? Sign me up...

There's just something about bad boys. Tattoos and leather jackets, am I right?

Trouble is, my last boyfriend was a teensy bit too bad and now he's in prison. Yikes.

When my friends challenge me to take a dip in the good guy side of the dating pool, I see their dating bet and I raise it, looking up the guy I crushed on growing up.

With a winning grin and heart of gold, Gabe Clements is now the star receiver for a pro football team.

Except, the supposed good guy turns out to be nothing like I imagined. He's better. He's growly, possessive, smoldering.

And he's determined too. At the end of the night, he asks me to be his **fake real girlfriend** for the rest of the week.

Sounds like my kind of dating challenge since he's a good guy by day, and a very dirty man after dark.

I'll cure my bad boy blues in no time.

Well, as long as I don't fall for Gabe's big heart too.

DID YOU KNOW?

By Lauren Blakely

To be the first to find out when all of my upcoming books go live click here!

PRO TIP: Add lauren@laurenblakely.com to your contacts before signing up to make sure the emails go to your inbox!

Did you know this book is also available in audio and paperback on all major retailers? Go to my website for links!

THE GOOD GUY CHALLENGE
BY LAUREN BLAKELY

Heat Warning! This book contains some seriously spicy scenes. All the sex is consensual, and if you want to know the type of kinks these characters enjoy, with safe words picked and verbal consent given, please go to my website. If you don't, proceed and get a fan!

MONDAY

A Day for Big Things Ahead

1

———

BETTER THAN A SCREAMING ORGASM

Ellie

I can see the sign for my Venice Beach exit up ahead, past all the cars at a dead stop. LA traffic...we'll move eventually. I'd be copacetic if I didn't have to pee so freaking badly.

Too bad I can't cross my legs as I drive.

I mean, as I wait.

I wiggle my rear, then I squeeze my thighs.

I can do this.

"We're almost there," I say to my girl in the back seat.

Gigi side-eyes me from her dog bed, a look that says *I don't buy that bullshit and you don't either.*

"I swear. We'll be there in no time."

Lies. Sweet little lies.

"Look, girlie girl. The GPS says we'll be there in"—I glance at the app mocking my hopes from the dashboard of the cherry-red convertible—"in thirty minutes."

I slump. Thirty minutes for one stinking mile.

She turns around, flipping her tail at me.

I get her. I so do.

"It'll be worth it, I promise. Once we're settled into our new home, it's going to be amazing. There's no snow in Los Angeles, and I'm pretty sure there won't be street rats," I say. God, I hope not. I'm so over rats, and subways, and piss on the street.

Dammit. Why did I have to think about pee again?

I stare longingly at the console between the seats, where my empty travel mug invites me to relieve the pressure.

Last resort, Ellie.

"Any minute. We'll be there any minute," I say, fighting off the temptation with cheer. "As long as I don't pee all over the seat. And don't you do that either," I warn my six-pound pup.

From the back seat, Gigi barks once, a declarative *arf* that loosely translates to *as if.*

"Fine, fine. It's my fault. I should not have had that last caramel iced latte in Santa Barbara, but TJ said it was a delish coffee shop and—oh!"

I turn forward to see that traffic has miraculously parted like the Red Sea. This is better than a screaming orgasm!

I grip the wheel and press the gas in my tricked-out electric, which I picked up in San Francisco over the weekend.

"We need a final song," I tell Gigi. Because life's big moments demand anthems, and I have just the tune. I open a playlist, then put "Runnin' Down a Dream" on repeat. Now there's no chance of another song playing when I roll up to my new home.

The sun is dropping toward the horizon, Tom Petty is my companion, and soon I'm cruising the streets of my Venice neighborhood, bursting—literally almost bursting—with excitement.

"One more minute till we can whiz," I sing. My phone trills an accompaniment.

Of course. I swear my mom has a sixth sense for my every move. I click accept. "Hi, Mom. How are you?"

"Much better now," she says with obvious relief.

That's odd. I talked to her this morning, and she seemed fine then. "Were you sick earlier? Everything okay?" I ask, concerned for her as I scan for street signs in my new neighborhood.

"No, just worried. About you."

Ah. Got it. "Nothing to worry about anymore. I'm

almost there. Only four-tenths of a mile to go." And my bladder is counting every fraction of that mile.

"I know," Mom says serenely.

I laugh. That is so her. It's sweet but scary how well she knows me. "I'm sure you timed exactly how many rest stops I'd take, how many coffees I'd down, and how many dog walks I'd stop for, and you guesstimated my average speed," I say as I slow to a stop at the intersection.

One more block. I can see my new street up ahead. Freedom is nigh!

"Two coffees, three dog bathroom breaks, and sixty-five to seventy miles per hour. Am I right?"

"Whoa. Did you put a chip in me?" I joke because that's impressive.

I tap the gas one more time.

She laughs like that's a loony thought. "Of course not. That's just mother's intuition," she says as I turn onto my new block. "I knew you got in okay because I've been tracking your location on Waze."

"Mom!" I shriek. That explains so much. "I told you not to stalk me anymore!"

"What? Everyone does it," she says as I scan the block of cottages for number 583.

"Everyone does *not* do it. Only helicopter moms do it."

"That's not true. Joanie tracks Mariana, Suzi tracks Taylor, and—"

"Helicopter moms," I repeat as I hit the blinker, the cute metal numbers for 583 calling me home.

"Ellie, sweetheart. You shared your location with me on Waze. I saved it. So sue me."

"I did that...years ago," I sputter. I was home from college for the summer, and it was the only way she'd let me borrow her car to go out with that sexy, tatted guy I met at a club.

"And imagine how hard it was for me to track your whereabouts when you were in New York for the past five years, walking everywhere, never using Waze. Thank god I can do it again. You should be grateful," she says, half teasing, half serious.

Wait. Make that *all* serious.

"I'm twenty-six, Mom." I pull into the driveway and cut the engine. "You can turn off the propellers."

"Ooh," she says brightly. "I see you officially reached your destination."

Are you kidding me? I stab the end drive button on my app, then turn it off. "Mom, that's me turning off the Waze."

"Don't turn off the sharing," she chides.

"Mom," I warn as I swing open the driver's side door. In record time, I unbuckle Gigi and grab her from the back seat, focused on getting the key from the lockbox and beelining to the little girls' room.

"Enough about me, though," Mom says as I

wrestle with the lockbox where Maddox left the key. "Have you heard the news?"

That's not foreboding at all. "What news?"

"It's about *Fabio's List*."

I groan in frustration, forgetting completely about my need to pee.

As I start this new chapter of my life, the last thing I want is a reminder of all my romantic failures.

2

UNSPANKED

Gabe

Five minutes, then I'm leaving, even if it is my home.

With her hands parked on her hips, and her gray eyes shooting death rays of *shame, shame, shame* at me, my ex's pissy big sister is building up a new head of steam. "Do you know how distraught my sister was by your freakish suggestion?" Jessica rants, pointing at the box of Brittany's stuff on the coffee table.

Of course I know. Everyone in my condo building knows, thanks to Brittany's ear-splitting outrage at my suggestion. *Hell no, I don't want you to spank me, you freak!*

But I'm not going to engage now because I want

my ex's sister to get the hell out of my pad. At this rip-me-to-shreds rate, I'm going to be late for poker and my buds will bust my balls.

"Honestly, I expected more of you," Jessica hisses, spewing more judgment at me. "You're an adult. You should behave like a gentleman."

"And your sister is a grown woman who said no and left here *unspanked,*" I say calmly, adding with a fake-ass smile, "So feel free to take her box and go."

I *wanted* to say *get the fuck out*, but I didn't. See? I am a gentleman.

Jessica grinds the spikes of her sling-back heels into my hardwood floor and glares at me, waggling a long black nail. "You should be ashamed."

"Britt made that quite clear," I say drily. My phone buzzes on the coffee table. It's probably Drew, docking points for me being late. I deserve that.

"You're thirty-six," Jessica spews. "Thirty-six-year-old men don't ask to spank their girlfriends."

I could beg to differ. I could also point out all the shitty things Brittany said to me while we were together, but instead, I grab the box and thrust it at her sister, hustling her toward the door. "Thanks for coming by. Here's the last of Brittany's things. Her poodle mug, her comfort-food cookbook, and her favorite spatula," I say.

"Good. I'm going to cook with her tonight to

make her feel better." She snatches the box. "She's still devastated by your outrageous request."

Jessica takes the box, then gasps, dropping it like it's on fire. "Ew! So gross."

"What?" I ask, eager to deal with her issue so I can get on with my evening.

With her mouth gaping, she points like the box is infected with...a spider? A snake?

I cross a few feet to the open box, then groan, annoyed when I see the issue.

A pair of silver gleaming handcuffs.

Jessica plucks the handcuffs out of the box with two disgusted fingers. "Brittany will *not* want these. You're just embarrassing yourself!"

Embarrassed is right, but not for the reasons Jessica thinks.

Embarrassed because I'd bought these to give Brittany for her birthday coming up. I even got a pink bow to tie around them. I'd been gearing up, too, to finally tell her why I wanted to play around with handcuffs. What I hoped it could do for us. How it might even help our relationship.

So, yeah, Jessica's tirade feels so fucking great right now.

"The cuffs can stay then," I say evenly. I don't want to let on that she's hitting below the belt. Taking the cuffs, I drop them on the entryway table.

Jessica raises an eyebrow all the way to Mars.

"You're keeping them? For what? The freak of your dreams?"

That's enough. I march ahead of her and swing open the door, then gesture to the hall. Somehow, I swallow down a *leave right fucking now.*

"Goodbye," I hiss.

She lifts a haughty chin. "Handcuffs," she mutters.

I bet someone will love them, I want to shout.

But I don't.

When she's gone, I slam the door shut. Once I hear the elevator whisk her away, I leave too. As I hit the button to call the next one, my next-door neighbor leaves her home. "Hold the elevator, handsome," the blue-haired lady calls out as she shuts her door.

"Anything for you, Myrtle," I say with a grin, then comply once the elevator arrives, hitting the hold button.

When she joins me a few seconds later, Myrtle tuts, shaking her head. "You're better off without the ex. She was nothing but trouble."

Thanks again, Brittany, for broadcasting my kink to the whole building.

"Thanks," I say. "It's good to be single again."

When we reach the lobby, Myrtle pats my arm. "And there's nothing wrong with a spanking. That's what I usually order on *Whipper.* In fact, I'm off to see a playmate right now."

Whoa. She uses *that* app? "Um, have fun," I say in a strangled voice.

She winks. "I always do."

I wish the last several months of my life had been fun, but I wasted them on someone who didn't even get me.

I swear I will never date a good girl again.

* * *

The guys are meeting up at my favorite haunt in Venice Beach, a local dive bar called The Happiest Hours right off the main drag, for my Free At Last poker party.

Drew and Axel—one's my quarterback, the other's his cousin—are at the table, and my buddy Milo is in town with his girlfriend, so he's here too. Drew said we need to celebrate my being single again. Far be it for me to turn down a chance to take their money.

Besides, "free at last" is right. Several months with Brittany felt like a lifetime. I frown at the cards in my hand. Does that make me forty-six? Ouch. I'll definitely be out of the NFL then. Don't want to go there any sooner than I have to.

Axel shoves a ten dollar chip into the pile on the

felt and offers an opinion for free. "I'm just going to be blunt. I never trusted Brittany anyway."

I look up from my cards, surprised. "Really? Why not? Did you catch her, I dunno, scrolling through Tinder some night while we were all out?"

Across the table, Axel stares at me and scoffs, "Seriously?"

Drew snorts. "Seconded. Get the fuck out, Gabe."

Milo gazes soberly over the top of his black glasses. "Dude, we would have told you if she'd done that. Keeping that kind of thing to yourself is grounds for expulsion from the dude club."

"True words," Axel confirms. "A lifetime ban."

"Good to know," I say, but I'm much more interested in what my buddy saw in my ex. We had a good vibe at first, which is why I was able to look past our sexual incompatibility. We had fun together, going to basketball games in the off-season. She seemed like the perfect sports girlfriend, and I did enjoy the hell out of trash-talking other teams from the stands with her.

Everything seemed good.

Until she started asking me questions about other women. Like, about the barista at the coffee shop we went to. *She keeps looking at you, Gabe,* she'd say. *Did you lead her on the last time you were here? Um, no.* Then, when we were out one night at a bar, my ex asked point blank if I was sleeping with the bartender who'd just batted her lashes at me.

The answer was *hell fucking no.*

"All right," I say to Axel. "What red flag did I miss?"

He deals me a hard, stern look—sort of his regular look but kicked up a notch. "When we all went to the Jane Black concert, she said irregardless. 'Irregardless of what you heard, Jane has a new song she's debuting tonight.' And—news flash—irregardless is not a word."

Drew cracks up, smacking the edge of the table. "Called it. I knew the *irregardless* would come back around and grind Axel's gears," he says, then wiggles his fingers toward Milo. "Pay up."

Milo sighs, aggrieved, then forks over a ten dollar chip. Drew uses it to add to the pot on the table.

I laugh, a little incredulous. "You assholes bet on whether Axel would mention that my ex used a word that didn't exist?"

Drew shrugs like *yeah, so,* then nods toward my playing cards. "What have you got? You in?"

Hell yes. I slide in a chip, then slap down the cards. "Three jacks. Which means…" I scoop the pile of chips my way. "I win. I'm free of my ex, and I'm beating your sorry asses. It's like a double victory."

"Damn right it is." Drew speaks with the same intensity he has in the huddle. "Don't date women who abuse the English language. You need a woman who reads. Like, a lot," he adds, with a thump on my shoulder and a wiggle of his brow. His fiancée is a big-time reader.

"I couldn't agree more," Axel says.

"Of course you'd say that. You're a writer," I point out.

"But I don't see you disagreeing, Gabe," Milo adds, then lowers his voice. "And you shouldn't. Because women who read are usually a lot more... *fun*."

There's a twinkle in his blue eyes. He doesn't sleep and tell—none of us do—but his message is clear.

A well-read woman is more fun in bed.

Hmm.

Maybe a bookworm would like to be bent over the bed, fastened to the headboard, or tied to a chair. Would take a hard smack to her ass and beg for more.

"I like fun," I deadpan as Drew gathers the cards. It's his turn to deal.

"Then maybe focus on that. We've got less than a week till training camp," Drew says, a leading tone in his voice as he brings up our trip to San Diego.

A week sounds perfect for a rebound. But if I go for a rebound, I don't want someone who'll shout *you kinky fucker* at me at the end of the week. It was bad enough the way Brittany stormed out. What if a woman comes up to me on the football field and does that for the media to hear? *Shudders.*

"It's my last year, though, so it's best that this old dog stays focused on the game," I say, with a resolute shrug. "No distractions."

"And sex is both distracting and dangerous, man. You could get injured screwing in the shower," Axel offers helpfully.

"Dude. Do you work to be a buzzkill, or does it come naturally?" I ask.

"I'm just saying. It's a thing. Be careful, old dog," Axel adds, with a smart-ass wink.

And ouch. Like I don't already know that, in football years, I'm as old as Yoda. "Hey, now. I don't want to hear about sex injuries till I'm way past forty. Maybe even fifty."

Drew sets down the deck and lifts his glass of beer. "Let's drink to staying healthy in your final year. No football injuries and no dick injuries. Just getting banged up on the field."

Laughing *and* rolling my eyes, I lift my beer and toast to football. At least *she* always likes it rough.

After taking a drink, I set the bottle on the table. As Drew shuffles the deck to deal the next round, my gaze strays to the window where a sexy-as-sin brunette chats on the phone as she walks a little dog down the street.

The woman's got a swing in her hips and a pouty fullness to her lips. She looks like a piece of candy, all effortlessly delicious in tight jean shorts, cut off and raggedy sexy, and a purple halter top that shows off her pierced belly. I'd like to peel that top off her, lick a path between her tits and down her stomach, then tug on her belly ring with my teeth. As I stare unabashedly a little longer, she starts to look damn familiar.

She reminds me vaguely of picnics, barbecues, Thanksgivings. Then, a Christmas party. A moment under the mistletoe, maybe.

Wait.

Hold the hell on.

Is that...?

No fucking way.

Another memory flashes before me of Ellie Snow. One of the times I babysat her.

3

A THING FOR BAD BOYS

Ellie

I dread calling my mom back, but I hung up on her when I got into my house. I used my pee-mergency as an excuse, but I'm a little freaked out over any news about my ex.

Still, I have to know the score. I grab a pair of pink flip-flops—with a flower between the toes—then shove my feet into them.

Except, this shirt is a little gross. I did drive in it all day. After a quick freshen up, I tug on a purple halter top, then leash up my leading lady and hit the road.

Our first walk in our new town. Too bad I'll have to use it to get the lowdown on my ex. But a girl's got to do what a girl's got to do. I stab Mom's contact name, my gut swirling with worry.

I'd heard rumors that LGO had picked up a series about my infamous ex-boyfriend—Dexter Longfellow, aka *Fabio*. The timing couldn't be worse professionally.

Mom answers on the first ring with a relieved sigh. "There you are. I was getting sick," she says.

"I was only gone for a few minutes," I reassure her as I turn down the block toward Abbot Kinney Boulevard. "What's going on with…" I gulp, then woman up and blurt out the name I wish I could avoid. "*Fabio's List.*"

"*The Hollywood Scoop* ran the piece today that LGO officially picked up the documentary. They're going to run it in the fall, the story says. Rikki Finch is the reporter, and she's never wrong." My mom is apologetic, as if it's her fault the show was greenlit.

My nerves speed through me like they're on the Jumbotron race car track at the ballpark. "Mom, do you think the producers are pissed that I turned down their request to do an interview for it? Can they mention me by name without my permission?"

"They better not, or they'll answer to me for it." I can picture her shaking a fist at the sky. Her mama-bear ferocity eases some of my worries. It always has. "But who'll want to watch this rubbish?" Mom continues. "Your show is going to be so much better," she assures me. "I have zero interest in viewing a salacious tell-all about a chiseled model who conned hundreds of thousands of dollars from women he found on dating apps. *Quelle horreur.*"

I clear my throat and lift my chin. "He didn't con me, though." I don't take just *some* solace in knowing that. I take *all* the solace in that.

"Of course not. I raised you right," Mom says proudly. "Still, I'm going to organize protests against the show. And you can focus all your energy on *The Dating Games.*"

The show I wrote and am producing for streaming giant Webflix starts shooting later this month. It's why I moved to Los Angeles. But the reality is, my last boyfriend went to prison for swindling women he met online. When word leaked a few months ago that a production company was shooting a salacious doc on his romantic duplicity for Webflix's rival, Hollywood tongues began wagging.

Right when I'm about to launch my new career, from actress to TV writer-slash-producer, the last thing I need is a trail of tawdry ex-shenanigans to follow me.

"I'll just say no if the producers ask me again," I say firmly. Like I said no to my ex when he told me he needed money because he was supposedly in danger. Some *bad guys* were after him, he'd claimed.

Please.

I kicked his ass to the curb, but I still don't want to appear on camera or be named as one of his exes. It's one thing for a few producers to know—quite another for all the industry. I want a clean slate as I start my new gig. It's hard enough to be taken seriously as a woman in Hollywood without a link to a scam artist.

"This is a sign you need to focus on dating good guys," Mom says, putting on her helpful tone.

Oh gee, that thought never occurred to me.

"Yes, Mom. I'm going to check the good-guy box on Boyfriend Material when I get on the apps in LA."

"I know you're rolling your eyes, but you have a habit of picking bad boys. It would be a good habit to try to break finally. Remember senior year when you dated that stoner who skipped school and stole money from me?" she points out.

"Yes, Mom," I concede begrudgingly. *But that stoner gave me my first O, and I was kinda hooked on Os after that.*

But there have been good guys in my dating repertoire—surely.

"And then in college, you went out with the guitarist from Astronaut Food. He had a permanent scowl. His fingers were inked. He rode a motorcycle, Ellie! A motorcycle! He was probably the president's son, like in a motorcycle club."

Someone has read too many MC romances. Besides, if she only knew...I've dated jackholes and jerkoffs too.

"I'll also check *guys who only drive station wagons*," I say as I head along Abbot Kinney with Gigi. My new neighborhood teems with trendy boutiques and quirky new eateries. This street buzzes with energy, brims with surfers and artists and athletes. Maddox set me up well.

"I'm just saying, those bad boy types are all over Los Angeles. Instead of joining a dating app, why don't you let me set you up when you come to Aunt Tilly's birthday party this weekend? There are some lovely guys here in San Diego. There's Chad, Joanie's son," she begins.

I blink. She can't mean that? "Chad literally just graduated from college." I tug my pup closer while a pack of skaters fly past us.

"But he's ready for a long-term commitment," Mom says.

Doubtful. More like Joanie wants him to settle down. "I'm not dating your friend's son. I can go solo to the party. That's a thing single people do."

She squeals. "Perfect. Then I can introduce you to everyone."

Oh god, no. That's worse. "I'll find a date," I say, cutting her plans off at the knees.

"Someone who doesn't keep a list of women he's scammed," she says, oblivious to the irony.

"Yes, Mom," I say as I pass a place called The Happiest Hours. It boasts a large window in the front. Through it, I catch a glimpse of a group of guys inside at a table in the corner. I can't see all of them, but one of them is *fiiiiine* from this angle.

I can just spy his profile, but he looks kind of familiar. Dark hair. Dark stubble. Dark eyes. Crinkles at the corner. Yum. Oh, and ink all over one arm.

Hello, wet panties.

I'm just saying.

Except, I'm sure he's trouble. Tempting. But trouble.

Must. Look. Away. After all, Mom was *just* talking about my preference for bad boys.

I activate all my powers of resistance and stop staring. Gigi and I leave him in the dust, turning toward our home. A few blocks later, I'm back at 583, where another hottie waits on my porch.

"At last, she's here," my friend Maddox calls out, and I rush and jump into his sturdy arms while Gigi barks enthusiastically at his feet.

Maddox is as strong as a tree, so he doesn't wobble, just laughs lightly. "Well, that's a helluva greeting," he says.

I drop to my flip-flopped feet and drink in my friend. In his aviator shades, tailored burgundy button-down, and pressed slacks, he looks every bit like the best sports attorney-slash-agent in the biz. We hit it off at an industry party years ago. The next week, we started training for a marathon together, and he's been my rock ever since.

"You're a godsend for finding me this rental. It's perfect. And I can't believe you got me a scooter too." I flap my arm toward the garage where I found his housewarming gift earlier.

"Glad you like it," he says.

"I love the scooter, and Gigi and I love this cottage, and to thank you, I want to take you out to dinner."

He gives a tender smile, the kind that I bet melts all the guys. "That sounds great, except that I'm taking *you* to dinner. Isn't that right, Gigi? I'm going to take your person out." He bends and scratches Gigi between the ears. She lifts her chin approvingly.

"But I want to treat." I pout. "You treated me to lunch when I was here a couple of weeks ago."

"And yet, it's still my turn." He straightens and crosses his arms, challenging me.

Damn him. He's stoic, and I know he'd wait all night and never break. I poke his firm biceps. "No wonder you're the toughest negotiator," I say.

"Your words..." he says, his smile teasing again.

"You know it's true." I let my girl inside and give her a quick kiss. "Back soon, lovie."

As we walk to dinner, I link my arm through my friend's. "Maddox, do you think I like bad boys?"

He scoffs. *Knowingly.*

"So, that's a yes?"

"You know you do, Ellie," he says, friendly but firm.

Maybe I do need to find that good-guy box on Boyfriend Material after all.

TUESDAY

A Day for the Naughty List

4

A PRIEST, A MONK, AND A MISSIONARY

Ellie

By the next morning, I'm eighty-two percent unpacked. Efficiency is kind of my thing. The entertainment industry is chock-full of unknowns and uncertainty, so staying on top of my daily life is necessary for my sanity.

Granted, I didn't lug much stuff cross-country from New York for my relo, partly because I rented a furnished home here. When I left my cute walk-up in Greenwich Village, I gave away my beloved purple couch to my neighbor and bestie, Veronica, and my bed to an actress friend. Then I shipped most of my clothes and books. As well as sex toys, overnight and fully insured, of course. Then I flew to San Francisco with my little lady on my lap. Gigi insisted on first-class travel, and I would never deny her. Or me, to be fair. After visiting my brother in Pacific Heights for a few days, I picked up my new electric wheels at a custom car shop, then drove the rest of the way here.

The little one-bedroom has plenty of space for Gigi and me, and I survey it happily. "I see you've already taken custody of the couch," I tell my critter, who's stretching out on the soft gray cushions. "You do know you were descended from wolves? Then you discovered couches."

She closes one eye, unamused. *Chihuahuas were descended from royalty, not wolves,* I imagine her saying.

She makes a reasonable point.

Everything looks good. I'm ready to hit the ground running. I have a slew of meetings later this week, with show production beginning next week. Today, though, I have all the time in the world to get to know my new hometown. The best part? Veronica is in LA for a client event, along with her sister, so I don't have to go into friend withdrawal yet.

After I shower and do my makeup, adding sparkly eye shadow because...why not, I tug on a little black cotton dress and lace up my pink Converse high-tops. Then I hop in my convertible to motor off to Santa Monica and meet my gal pals for breakfast.

When I find Veronica and her sister, Hazel, at a sidewalk table at The Tree House, the Pacific Ocean crashing majestically far on the other side of the street, I greet them like it's been years.

"Don't ever leave me again," I tell Veronica, octopussing my arms around her.

"Ahem. You left me," Veronica corrects when we finally separate. "You revisionist historian, you."

"I'm the worst," I agree, then I wrap Hazel in a hug too. "Maybe you should move to Los Angeles. Join me here, Hazel. Do it, do it, do it."

She shakes her head, her red locks swishing back and forth. "New York suits my cold, black heart."

"Truer words," I say with a wink, then slide into the booth. After we order—tofu scramble for this aspiring vegan—I turn to my brunette bestie, squeezing Veronica's hand. "For the record, it's been less than a week and I miss you terribly. I don't know how I'll survive without living across the hall from you. I might start a GoFundMe to move you and Milo here to Los Angeles, ideally Venice Beach, and preferably to the house next to mine."

"You've already picked out a new home for them in Los Angeles?" Hazel asks with a huff. "Great. Just great. Now I'll never see my sister again."

Veronica shoots me a curious smile. "Tell me more about this house next to yours. Does it have a balcony? A pool? Any other amenities that would lure me away from New York? Though, there is that little matter of Milo's shop being in, you know, New York City."

Yeah, that's the flaw in my plan—her beau's burgeoning bike and flower shop located smack dab in Manhattan. "Then please consider learning tele-portation. It would make my life easier. Or try to land as many Date Night for One parties in Los Angeles as possible," I suggest, since I'm helpful like that. Plus, I'm a huge fan of Date Night for One's subscription boxes for sex toys, since, well, I like toys.

Veronica's green eyes pop. "Oh! You should come to my party this week. The woman hosting it runs a jewelry shop in Venice Beach full of local female artists. Her name is Rachel, and she and some of the other women-owned businesses are throwing the party for their customers."

I wiggle a brow. "Girl, you had me at sex toys."

"Ellie's easy like that," Hazel chimes in drily as the server arrives with our coffees and teas.

We thank him, and Veronica shifts moods shooting me a serious look. "How are you doing with the *Fabio's List* news?"

I cringe. "I was hoping to bury my head in the sand. But since I can't, I'm doing okay. Though, Mama Snow *hounded* me hard about my dating habits yesterday. She wants to set me up with all her friends' sons. She thinks that'll help me"—I sketch air quotes—"break the bad boy habit." Then I sigh, resigned. "She's probably not wrong. Dexter *is* in prison."

Veronica smiles sympathetically. She's too nice to agree, but her silence says I need to go to reform school. Then, she clears her throat. "Maybe you could turn over a new leaf in Los Angeles?" she suggests.

Oh! And she's not too nice after all! But I need a kick in the pants. "I know," I admit, then take a sip of my coffee. "But how? How the hell do I just find a nice guy? It's hard enough to date these days. The whole premise of my TV show is the games people play when dating."

Hazel hums, a sure sign the romance novelist is planning a plot twist for me. "I have an idea," she says, sounding deliciously clever, which she is. "I was listening to a dating podcast, and it's all about turbo-boosting your dating life with different challenges. It reminds me of your show a little bit. And one of the ideas is if you're seeing someone, you try three dates where you come up with new places to go—pickling carrots, kite flying, candle sniffing."

Veronica arches a brow. "Candle sniffing is a thing?"

"Everything is a thing," Hazel says, then zooms on down Idea Lane. "And there are other challenges.

Like, challenge yourself to swipe right on three guys who are out of your comfort zone."

"So, for me, that'd be a priest, a monk, and a missionary?"

Veronica laughs. "Ellie, why do I suspect you've already defrocked a priest at some point in your life?"

I knit my brow, cycling back through my past loves. "I wish. I've had some seriously hot priest fantasies," I admit.

Hazel gives me a look that says *so not surprised* then marches onward. "So the challenge for you, Ellie, would be to avoid hot priests, because that's a recipe for trouble." She nibbles on the corner of her lips, then her eyes twinkle. "I've got it! By the power vested in me as one of your girlfriends, I challenge you to go on one date with a good guy."

Ooh, I do love a challenge. "So this is the Good Guy Challenge?"

"Yes, do it, Ellie," Veronica urges.

"But how do I find him?" I ask, instantly intrigued. I would like to change my fortune.

"Is there someone you know? Maybe from high school or college?" Veronica suggests, then lifts her cup of chai tea and takes a drink.

"I studied theater. Most of the guys were gay."

"Fair point," Veronica says, then taps her chin. "And your actor friends?"

"I don't like to mix business and pleasure. It's hard enough as a woman trying to make it in Hollywood," I say. "That's why I started scriptwriting. I didn't want to face the inevitable invisibility that comes with turning thirty-five, watching roles dry up, except for the mom, the teacher, or the gay guy's best female friend. On the flip side, a man can bang anyone as long as he's still standing, even if he needs a cane or a walker."

"Amen," Veronica agrees. "But back to the challenge. Who do you know outside of Hollywood?"

"Hmm. I need someone I can take home to Mom," I muse, picturing the birthday party coming up for Aunt Tilly. Hosted at my mom's house—the home where I grew up.

Oh!

An image pops into my head.

The guy who lived down the street from me growing up. He was older than me, and he used to help all the moms with yard work and chores. "I know! Gabe Clements," I say.

Hazel tilts her head. "The football player? As in, the receiver for the Los Angeles Mercenaries?"

"Yes," I say.

"Oh, that's right. When we watched that game last year, you said *that's my sexy next-door neighbor.*"

I sure did. I enjoyed the hell out of watching Gabe play football. Every time I saw him rip off his helmet, I had heart palpitations. His eyes made my stomach flip even through the TV screen.

"Gabe's perfect for the challenge," I say, jazzed by this idea already. "He's the consummate good guy. He helped all the moms. They always cooed about what a sweetheart he was, bringing their trash cans back from the street, mowing their lawns, and so on. My mom always went on and on about what a good guy he was."

"He sounds great then," Hazel says.

He sure does.

But I have other memories of Gabe, more private ones. Ones I don't share with my friends.

Like when I was fifteen and home alone on a Saturday in May. My parents took my sister and brother to the Santa Barbara baseball tournament for the day. But the game went into extra innings, so they decided to snag a hotel room. They asked Ms. Clements to send her son to spend the night so I wouldn't be alone in the house.

That was the hardest *and* the hottest night ever. The sexy football star slept fully clothed on the living room couch downstairs while I tossed and turned under the covers in my second-floor bedroom, hot and bothered, imagining the then twenty-five-year-old stud stalking upstairs and fucking me into my twin bed.

Of course, nothing of the sort happened. Gabe is,

as advertised, a good guy.

But it didn't stop my younger lustful self from dreaming.

I smile. Wickedly. Yes, I will definitely take the good-guy challenge for Gabe Clements.

5

FILL HER STOCKING

Gabe

The next morning, I work out with Drew at the Mercenaries stadium, running routes with my quarterback. As he rolls through the playbook, I am in the zone, focused on football only.

That's how I plan to be this season.

Like when I haul in a beautiful spiral and take it to the end zone.

When Drew catches up with me, I give a cocky shrug. "Guess we're ready for the Super Bowl."

"'Course we are," he says, then with the ball tucked under my arm, we head to the corridor.

"What's it like?" he adds. "To win one?"

I smile at the glorious memory of a certain

Sunday a few years ago. Even now, I get a chill. A good chill, just thinking of how it felt to claim the Lombardi trophy. "You know how great sex is?"

Drew snorts, then laughs. "Yeah. I do."

"Imagine something one hundred times better than that," I say.

He whistles. "Damn."

"And then you're *maybe* in the ballpark."

"You fucker," he mutters.

"You asked," I toss back. Then, I clap him on the shoulder. "We're gonna have a good year. It's my personal mission to make a ring happen. I got your back."

"And I've got yours," he says and then we head to the weight room inside the facility.

While I work out, I try to focus on football only.

With every chest press, I zoom in on the season I want to have, the plays I want to make, the stats I want to surpass.

But somewhere between the squats and the lat raises, my mind returns to the vision from last night in a purple halter top and short shorts that revealed a hint of cheek.

I've run into Ellie a few times over the past several years. Ellie's grandma's birthday extravaganza a year ago. Then last summer at the fortieth-anniversary party my brother and I threw our mom and dad.

Ellie brought them a board game to celebrate the occasion because my parents met at a Monopoly tournament and have always loved their game nights.

But my most vivid memory is when I saw Ellie under the mistletoe at my aunt Sarah's eggnog-tasting party five years ago. Resisting kissing her was harder than catching a Hail Mary pass.

Ellie was in college then, twenty or twenty-one, batting those big brown eyes at me and smiling up at the sprig of mistletoe. She was all sweet innocence with only a slash of red lipstick across her bee-stung mouth to hint at dirty deeds.

"Merry Christmas, Gabe," she'd said in her smoky, sexy voice. "Have you been a good boy this year?"

No. I had not. Not one bit.

"I always am," I said. "What about you?"

She shrugged coquettishly. "I skipped a seminar last week. I hope that doesn't get me on the naughty list."

I'd like to get on that list with her.

"That doesn't seem like enough of a sin," I said.

"Oh," she said, with a wicked glint in her eyes. "Maybe I should try harder."

I *was* harder.

"Guess it depends if you want presents from Saint Nick," I said, trying to be friendly, not flirty. I couldn't tear myself away from her, even though I should have.

"I do like gifts. Maybe Santa will understand. I sure hope he'll fill both our stockings," she'd said.

Her stocking wasn't what I wanted to fill. I'd balled my hands into fists, resisting my mom's friend's daughter and the urge to wipe off all that lipstick with a hard, punishing kiss.

Especially when she waited, chin tipped up, under the mistletoe.

I swallowed down the surge of lust. She was in college, for fuck's sake.

Then she smiled, bright and big. Sweet as cherry pie.

I relaxed, seeing again the sweet girl next door. She wasn't the Christmas vixen on the naughty list.

"And to all a good night," I said, then she rose onto her tiptoes and brushed a chaste kiss to my cheek.

Then, thoroughly innocent, she walked straight to the eggnog bar and chatted with her mom.

Innocent. Sweet. Friendly.

That was who she was.

That's probably who she still is.

Even though those words—*naughty list*—echo in my mind years later. Along with the way she flirted with me.

She's probably the consummate good girl. But...

what if she's not? What if her naughty list comment was a hint?

The possibility is too enticing. I've got to know if that was even her last night. She *was* walking a dog, after all. You don't usually walk a dog when you're just visiting. Has she moved to Los Angeles from New York?

No harm, no foul in finding out, right?

I let go of the lat-raise bar, climb off the machine, and grab my water bottle. As I take a glug, I glance around. Drew's lifting free weights, so I can snag a moment to check her out. I slip my phone from my shorts pocket, unlock it, and search for Ellie Snow.

Her social media feed, full of pics, pops up right away.

And so does my dick.

Just look at those tits. Those lips. That stomach.

She's no longer the off-limits teenage girl down the street. She's not the college beauty either. She's all woman, and she has filled the fuck out in the rack department.

Hips too.

I could grip those hips hard. Grab a fistful of that chestnut hair. Devour those candy lips.

Like a detective cracking the case, I tap the screen with a satisfied grin. Yup. She's got a little blond dog, just like the gal strutting past The Happiest Hours.

"I knew it," I mutter, victorious.

"Knew what?"

Busted. Drew's behind me, peering over my shoulder. I stuff my phone into my pocket right away. He stares as if he caught me red-handed, which he did. "So, it seems you *aren't* so worried about non-football injuries," he teases.

I huff, rolling my eyes. "Just looking someone up. No big deal." I nod to the StairMaster. "I need to hit the steps."

"Is that the only thing you need to hit?"

I flip him the bird.

No matter how appealing the idea of hot rebound sex is, I'm still reeling from the *here's your handcuffs* moment.

Sure, Ellie flirted her sweet ass off with me at a Christmas party a few years ago. But no way do I want to screen Ellie, or anyone, with questions like—*so, want it rough, dirty and, maybe, bound?*

Best to stick to the football-only plan. I blast a hard-rock playlist as I sweat on the StairMaster.

I don't reach out to Ellie. Then I truly do my best to put her out of my mind.

When I return home from the gym, the handcuffs on the entryway table catch my eye.

Damn my ex.

I pick them up and slide a finger across the shining metal, a latent irritation stirring inside me. I'm not annoyed that I didn't get to use them. I'm annoyed that I didn't even get a chance to *talk* to Brittany about why I wanted to. With the way she'd been needling me—unfairly—about other women, I wanted to show her she was the only one I thought of. That we could spice it up in the bedroom. Test some limits.

But I didn't even get to have that convo with her.

Now I'm left with unused cuffs. Good cuffs. Be a real shame to toss them into the trash. Maybe I can donate them to a charity for so-called *perverts* in need.

Or maybe...

Cuffs in hand, I leave my pad and head down the hall to knock on Myrtle's door. When she answers, her wise eyes widen. "Hey, handsome. It's a good thing you came by. I need a tall drink of water to reach the suitcase on my highest shelf."

"Happy to help," I say, then clear my throat, avoiding eye contact as I dangle the cuffs. "I was wondering if you might be able to give these a good home?"

Her eyes spark, and she grabs them faster than I haul in footballs. "I most certainly can. And I will put them to good use this weekend. I have a retreat," she says, leading me to her hall closet.

"What kind of retreat?" I ask as I easily snag her roller bag from the top shelf.

"A Whipper Retreat. It's a kink workshop. You only live once, as they say," she says.

"Words to live by," I reply.

I return to my condo, considering Myrtle's words of wisdom as I flop onto my couch. I return to Ellie's social feed, curious, so damn curious, about this sexy beauty.

Is she still the girl next door, sweet as vanilla? Or is she the kind of woman who likes to play?

I stare at the pic of her and her dog for another minute. Then I spot a reply to my...*heart?*

Oh, shit. I guess I hit like on her pic. Her reply is simple and far too tempting.

Hey, you...

Fuck screening her.

I send her a DM.

6
____

VERY BIG BINOCULARS

Gabe: Hey to you too…I'd say it's been a while, but I'm pretty sure that was you in the purple halter top and jean shorts walking past me last night.

Ellie: Oooh, are you spying on me?

Gabe: Maybe I am. Want to test my spy skills?

Ellie: Absolutely. Can you tell me what I'm wearing right now?

Gabe: Pink. Lots of pink.

Ellie: Those are some very big binoculars, mister.

Gabe: Huge.

Ellie: So you saw me last night and didn't even say hi, Gabe? Way to make a gal feel welcome in her new town.

Gabe: Should I send you a welcome basket? With fruits and candles and stuff?

Ellie: Hmm. Tell me more about this *stuff*.

Gabe: Decadent dark chocolate? Champagne? A fine wine?

Ellie: Stuff, please!

Gabe: Excellent. Now I know how to make you feel welcome.

Ellie: Well, that's a start. ;)

Gabe: Noted. And last night, in my defense, the window at The Happiest Hours got in the way.

Ellie: Should have broken it down.

Gabe: Next time. But damn, your dog is cute. Also, those were some nice shorts, Ellie.

Ellie: Same to you...for the tattoos and stubble, that

is. I thought that might have been you. Now I know it was.

Gabe: Who's the spy now?

Ellie: Well, you're not wearing a shirt at the moment, so I guess I am too.

Gabe: Are you stationed in the building across from mine, keeping watch on me?

Ellie: Do you want me to be?

Gabe: I don't have much more to take off, so I suppose the answer is yes.

Ellie: If you were dressed, would the answer be no?

Gabe: Come to think of it, the answer would still be yes. By the way, I was going to ask if you're living in Los Angeles now, but your social gave me the answer when I looked you up.

Ellie: I guess the jean shorts were memorable enough to go searching.

Gabe: The whole package was unforgettable, Ellie.

And welcome to Los Angeles. I hope you and Gigi like it here.

Ellie: Nice move, remembering my dog's name. Funny, I was looking you up this morning too.

Gabe: Oh yeah? Any reason in particular?

Ellie: I have my reasons. But why don't you go first and tell me why you looked me up. Just the shorts?

Gabe: How about I tell you tonight? Any chance you're free for dinner? Or drinks? Or a dog walk?

Ellie: Let's start with a drink.

Gabe: Meet me at eight. Gin Joint is a new lounge bar in Venice. Great drinks, great vibe.

Ellie: Are jean shorts a requirement?

Gabe: Wear anything. Or nothing.

Ellie: Funny, I was going to say the same to you.

7

MY TEENAGE WET DREAM

Ellie

This is just drinks. I only want to prove I'm not a bad-boy magnet. And if this date with a certified good guy goes well, perhaps he can be my plus one for Aunt Tilly's party, complete with apple pies, lemonade, and lawn croquet—in pairs, of course. Mom and her sisters love a good lawn party. If Gabe goes with me, that'll keep Mom from hounding me about my taste in men.

Gabe's like a mom shield. That's all.

I check my reflection in the full-length mirror in my bedroom. Cotton-candy pink ribbed tank, a black distressed jean skirt, and zip-up ankle boots.

Damn, I like the way I look. I bet he will too. The man seems to like pink. No reason *not* to lean into his color preferences.

I flip my head over, fluff my hair a final time, then pop back up in a cloud of chestnut waves. Yup, I'm ready to see my teenage wet dream.

A flare of excitement lights up inside me, but I do my best to keep it in check.

I don't want to get too caught up in my girlhood crush.

This is just drinks.

I focus on the practical details. Gin Joint is about a mile away, so I'll ride my scooter. I can have a drink and not worry about driving home. Grabbing my little shoulder bag, I leave the bedroom then find my fave four-legged person in the living room, this time curled up on her red velvet dog chair like a little queen. "Don't get into trouble while I'm gone," I tell Gigi.

She looks like she's saying: *I'm perfect, don't you know?*

"Yes, I do know that," I say, then bend over her throne to tap her little wet nose. She licks my face, letting me know she forgives me for even suggesting she'd be less than a lady while I'm gone.

I head to the garage, tapping a note to Maddox on my phone as I go. **Guess what I'm doing tonight? Taking the scooter you got me as I head out on a date!**

His reply is instant. *A date with a bad boy?*

I laugh, shaking my head. He'll be so proud of me. *I'm turning over a new leaf. I'm taking a good guy out for a spin. So there.*

Enjoy the ride. And of course I mean the...guy.

As I sling on my helmet, I write back: *Maddox, who's bad now?*

Then I tuck the phone away and dial into the moment.

Not the past and my long-ago lust for Gabe Clements. But the present and the challenge. As I ride through the neighborhood streets, I imagine leaving a trail of bad boys in the dust.

I'm living in a new town where I'm going to be a new woman. A woman who knows how to pick 'em. Not a woman who gets tangled up with cons, jerks, and thieves.

I turn onto the busy main road, then park on the sidewalk outside Gin Joint, hop off the scooter, and unsnap the helmet. I peer in the window, fluffing my hair.

But before I push open the door to the too-cool lounge, the butterflies flap wildly in my chest.

Again.

I'm about to have a drink with the guy I harbored a wicked, forbidden crush on when I was in high school. Back then, I was fifteen. He was twenty-five. He was all kinds of off-limits, and yet Gabe Clements sleeping on my parents' couch in all his muscly, bearded glory was my goddamn sexual awakening when I was busy growing boobs.

Well, I sneaked downstairs, of course and watched him sleep. I had no choice!

The butterflies race through me, kicking up naughty fantasies again.

Oh, hell.

What have I done?

Gabe might be a sweetheart, but there's no way I can make it through an evening with the man without blurting: *Do you know how many orgasms I imagined you giving me while I was under my polka-dot comforter late at night?*

The answer? Countless.

But the man wasn't only my teenage crush. He was my college fantasy too. When I saw him at his aunt's eggnog-tasting party, I pictured him throwing me over his shoulder and stalking up the stairs, then manhandling me against the door of her guest room.

Stop, Ellie. Just stop.

I can't linger on those dirty dreams.

I'm simply going to act...cool, casual, and totally unruffled by the filthy forbidden fantasies of my younger years.

I head into the speakeasy. Sensual lounge music greets me, a tune about how longing can drive you mad. It's the kind of song you listen to on a hot afternoon as the fan rattles overhead, and you pour a stiff drink while lingering on thoughts of a lover.

Not helpful, sound system.

I should have suggested an alternative to Gin Joint. Counter offered with the Surf Shack or Tony's Beachside Darts and Brew. Something easy with fries and margaritas and sunlight.

Gin Joint is low lights, pulsing music, and plush velvet couches. It's foreplay.

But I've got this. I'm *Reformed Ellie* tonight, and I'm on a good-guy mission.

I avoid the chaise lounges and head straight for the bar. The bar is safer than the inch-closer-to-me vibe of the couch. As I weave past couples and groups of guys and gals, I'm hunting for the six-foot-three, broad-shouldered, steel-chested football player. But I don't see Gabe, so I set my helmet on the bar, grabbing a stool at the end of the sleek metal counter. I'll just take a moment to catch my breath before he comes in.

As I hop up on a black stool, a big hand spreads across my lower back, right below my tank.

On my exposed flesh.

It could be any guy, but instinctively, I know it's Gabe.

Big and strong.

Then, as his fingers tug on the end of my tank, a deep, growly voice floats past my ear. "Better than jean shorts."

So much for Cool Ellie. I'm already lava hot.

8

─────

EARLY BEDTIME

Ellie

I turn to face my good-guy date, breath hitching as I take in his dark, broody eyes, and his lush lips.

Then, the rest of him.

And Gabe looks *gooooood* in well-worn jeans that hug his thighs and a black T-shirt that stretches deliciously over his pecs. Not too tight and saying *look at me*, but not too loose and saying he doesn't care.

The whole casual ensemble is just right for this Goldilocks.

His T-shirt hits his biceps, showing off the ink on his right arm. His skin is lined with black art, from flames to abstract geometric designs, with stars and sunbursts curving over and under the fine lines.

A well-designed sleeve makes me murmur *oh, yes.*

My curious gaze travels to his face once more. His mouth is sinful, and his dark chocolate brown eyes are already undressing me.

"You look good, Ellie Snow," he says, in a sexy rasp that makes the hair on my arms stand on end. "And I knew pink would be just your color."

My brain goes haywire with lust.

I swallow, searching for words, but my libido hid them all. I need to speak soon.

As in...*now.*

"Um, your jeans are nice too," I blurt out.

What kind of drivel was that? *Your jeans are nice?* Am I fifteen again?

He spreads his fingers across my back, making a statement. *Mine.* "Glad you like them. Want a drink?"

A drink. Yes! I can do this. I can order something.

Except what do I like to drink? I can't remember.

Help, universe! Help!

A Shirley Temple? A Coke?

Somewhere in the back of my mind, words form, and I grab them, spitting out, "A piña colada would be nice."

I cringe. I wouldn't blame the place for barring me. But the truly mortifying thing isn't that I had just asked for grandma's beach cocktail in a place called *Gin Joint.* It's the vivid memory of fifteen-year-old me trying to Lolita my way over to him in the kitchen like I did when he offered to make mac and cheese the second time he babysat. Instead, I jokingly asked for a piña colada because it was the only drink I knew of, and somehow, I thought that'd make me sound sexy to him.

But Gabe simply flashes me a charming, confident smile, then says, "A virgin one, Ellie?"

Like he'd said that night, calling me on my bluff.

He's only going to see me as a little girl. Too young to date.

Is there a start-over button somewhere, please? "Can you excuse me for a second?" I ask, then I scurry to the ladies' room. After I shut the door, I press my palms to the counter, then talk back to my reflection.

Get your act together. He's not the off-limits, sexy lawn guy from down the street anymore. He's an NFL receiver, and you're a successful actress turned writer. You might have once had a filthy crush on this sweetheart of a man, but you don't need to act like you're fifteen and he's forbidden fruit.

You're on a date.

I take another breath, reapply my lip gloss, then return to the bar. When I reach Gabe, I give him a smile and a smidge of the truth. "So, I apologize for my evil twin sister who started this date poorly on my behalf. I've kicked her to the curb and it's just me now. To answer your question, I'd love a chardonnay."

Gabe grins, the cocky lopsided kind of grin that makes my stomach flip, then sets a hand on my back again, heating me up once more. "Too bad about your twin sister. But I like both of you," he says in a dirty whisper.

Tingles race down my chest. "Good to hear," I murmur.

With his free hand, he calls the bartender over. "Hey man," he says with a charming smile. That must be his PR grin, the one he uses for the sports media. "How's it going? You having a good night?"

"I am," the guy behind the bar says. "What can I do for you?"

Gabe looks at me, running his hand possessively over my back. "*My date* would like a chardonnay, and I'll take a bourbon."

I squirm a little bit in my seat, stifling a smile at the claim.

"Coming right up," the man says, then spins around to grab glasses.

Gabe returns his focus to me. "So the piña colada comment, Ellie. Tell me something," he says, his tone a little demanding.

"Yes?"

"Do I make you nervous?"

More like nervous and hot. But I'm not ready to be *that* candid.

I do admit, "You did at first, but then I realized you're a good guy, and I shouldn't be nervous around you."

I looked him up because he's the opposite of my ex. He's good and charming. He's the boy next door.

Okay, the *guy* next door. Or that's the idea.

His lips curve upward in intrigue. "Is that so?"

"You always helped everyone around the neighborhood. Our block was filled with the prettiest lawns. And I seem to remember you made the best mac and cheese," I say, giving him a flirty smile.

"Ah, so you like me for my gardening. Duly noted," he says, and when the bartender returns with our drinks, Gabe thanks him. A couple of guys walk toward us, the mustached one staring at my chest. Gabe glowers at the guy, and he snaps his gaze away.

With that leer vanquished, Gabe smiles at me, then lifts his glass. "To you," he says.

I lift mine. "To you looking me up," I say, clinking with his tumbler.

"Or to you looking *me* up," he teases.

Finally. We're flirting in a way I can handle.

"Hey, now. You were going to tell me why *you* looked me up. I'm still waiting," I say with a smile, then I take a sip of my wine, and he knocks back some bourbon.

"Ladies first," he says.

Fine. If I must. Best to put this out in the open anyway. "My friends challenged me to go on a date with a good guy," I say, laying out the truth and nothing but. It's easier than playing games. I don't have it in me to toy with him. Not after I stumbled out of the gate.

He inches closer to me. "Of all the men in Los Angeles, you picked me for this experiment?"

"Did I pick badly?" I counter innocently, fluttering my lashes. Yes, I'm getting my groove back.

He lifts his glass, saying nothing, then swallows some liquor. "I'll surprise you by the end of the night, Ellie," he says in a smoky tone.

My stomach flutters. "Good. I love surprises."

"Me too. But tell me more about this...*good guy challenge*," he says, his gaze locking on mine.

"No, it's your turn." I touch his arm and let my fingers settle there. I'm totally copping a feel, and Gabe knows it, judging by the way he glances down at my hand then back up to meet my eyes.

"You said you'd tell me why you looked me up," I prompt, reminding him of our texts from earlier. "Don't leave a gal hanging."

He lets out a satisfied breath, like he's glad I asked. "When I saw you last night, I remembered that Christmas party at my aunt's house when you were in college. Remembered the mistletoe.

Thought about what I'd wanted to do to you that night."

This is no longer playful flirting. This is hot, racy, dirty talk, headed only one direction. I grip the edge of the bar so I don't climb him right here. Trying to keep my cool, I look up at the empty space above our heads. "But there's no mistletoe here, Gabe."

When our eyes meet again, his smile comes at me like a seduction, slow and sensual. "The night is young, Ellie," he says, in a voice hinting that maybe he's not so nice.

Then he shifts his tone to something less incendiary. "So you're here in Los Angeles."

I'm grateful for the change in topic. I was about to melt like a popsicle onto the floor. "I moved here for work. I had a great new opportunity on a show I wrote and am producing."

I raise my glass for another sip, and as the wine slides past my lips, I spot a ginger-haired man walking toward us, his gaze lingering on my face as if he recognizes me, maybe from the TV show I acted in?

The redhead slows as he gets closer to me, and the sound that comes from Gabe's throat is feral. A low, menacing growl, like a dog.

Aimed at the man.

Holy fuck.

Is that hot?

Yes, that is hot.

The guy passes us, weaving into the crowd. Once he's gone, Gabe's focus turns back to me. Completely.

"Do you like the new job?" he asks, as if he didn't just turn part wolf a second ago.

Okay, so we're doing it this way. "I'm sure I will. We begin table reads and stuff next week, and I start meeting with Webflix for prep tomorrow."

"Then I shouldn't let you stay out too late," he says, with a naughty curve to his lips.

"I suppose I *should* behave and go to bed early," I say, then cross my legs and sit higher, straighter, like a very good girl.

He laughs softly. "So, it seems you think I'm a good guy. Does that mean you like good guys, Ellie?"

"That's the question, isn't it?" I ask.

I'm a little unsure now of the answer, though. I thought he was this sweetheart. He had a reputation in the neighborhood as the kind of guy you'd take home to meet your mother.

At least, that was what I'd heard back home. Except the moms didn't know *this* Gabe. They knew kind, helpful Gabe. They had no idea he's got an intense, possessive side. A side that growls like he'd rip the head off anyone who looked at me the wrong way.

My pulse spikes at the thought, so I give my

answer an addendum. "So I guess I'll just surprise you too."

He slides his arm around me and squeezes my waist. "Sweetheart, you are full of surprises," he says.

His fingers are kindling. They stoke the flames inside me. My skin turns hot. I can't believe I thought lawn games would be Gabe's speed.

Maybe I'll ask him after I finish this glass. We turn to small talk about my new home, and when I finish my wine, I excuse myself for the ladies' room, heading down the dark corridor in the back to freshen up.

But after I wash my hands and leave the bathroom, the red-haired man is waiting for me in the dimly lit hall, right across from the ladies' room.

My guard goes up.

"Aren't you Ellie Snow?" he asks, stepping closer, his tone pushy.

Warning bells sound.

"Yes, I am," I say, putting on a polite but distant smile as I quickly assess the fastest way to escape him.

But he stands between me and the exit. It's a level three now. His eyes travel over my body in an unwelcome tour, and I cross my arms protectively.

"I had such a crush on you in *Unfinished Business*," he says. "Never missed an episode. Any chance you'd want to go out with—"

"Not a chance in hell. She's with me."

Like a superhero appearing out of nowhere, Gabe's laying down the law as he stalks down the corridor, prowling toward the man.

My heart beats in my throat. But whether it's from the thought of what the guy might do or Gabe might do, I don't even know.

The redhead holds up his hand. "Chill, man. I didn't know you were with her."

"The fuck you didn't," Gabe growls. "You saw her with me at the bar."

"Dude. Back off," the guy says defensively. "She smiled at me. I figured she wanted to meet me too."

Seriously? "I was being polite," I say, incredulous.

"She's polite. You're not." Gabe gets up in the guy's face now.

"You could let her make her own decisions," the man says to Gabe.

Another growl. "It's not an advanced concept, man. Just basic decency. Don't hit on a woman in the dark back hallway of a bar, especially when she's on a date with another man." Then he turns to me, asking, "Or, gee, sweetheart. Am I wrong? Did you want his number?"

I shake my head, reining in a grin because he's not joking. The grin is because he looks deadly serious about enforcing my decision, whatever it might be.

Gabe turns back to the man. "There. You heard it from her. Leave. And stay the fuck away from another man's date. *She is mine.*"

I'm not grinning now. I've been heating up since he appeared in the corridor. The quickened heartbeat from earlier? Now I feel a rapid ache. And I am soaked.

The man deflates and mumbles, "Sorry," to Gabe, who points to me.

"You were rude to her. Tell *her* you're sorry."

"Sorry," the guy says to me, dipping his face.

"Thanks," I say, then he rushes past Gabe with his tail between his legs.

Gabe watches till he's gone then turns to me, jaw ticking, dark eyes flaring with heat and residual anger.

"You shouldn't have to deal with that shit," he says, his voice tight, "whether you're with me or alone."

I lick my lips. "But I'm with you tonight," I whisper.

"Damn right you are," he says.

My skin sizzles. My pulse surges. "So I'm yours?"

His eyes glimmer with desire. All his annoyance seems to have vanished. He closes the distance, grabs my wrists, then pins them behind my back. He presses his strong, big frame against mine, his hard-on grinding against my hip.

Dear god.

"Yes, you are," he growls.

I wait for him to come for my lips.

But instead, he lays a hot, hungry kiss on the hollow of my throat.

I moan.

When he pulls back, he says, "Want to know why I looked you up?"

"I do," I say, breathless.

"Because you're finally old enough that I can ask the next question."

"What is it?"

His eyes roam up and down my face, my tits, my legs. I'm pretty sure he's already undressed me mentally. Pretty sure, in his mind, his face is between my thighs right now.

He stares hotly at me, then asks, "Can I take you home and fuck you?"

So I was wrong. It's not his face between my legs. And I'm more than okay with that.

I gasp out a throaty "yes."

9

HANDY LESSONS

Gabe

I got carried away back at the bar. Came on too strong and demanded too much. Now I'm walking Ellie home, with her slowly riding her scooter beside me, and my brain's taken over the thinking from my dick once more.

I have a whole mile to contemplate all the ways that sleeping with the too-sweet Ellie Snow is a terrible idea. It'd be a mistake at a basic level, screwing a family friend, someone I'll see at Christmas parties, at picnics, at Thanksgivings. I just ended a long-term relationship where my ex and I were woefully incompatible in the bedroom. I *knew* she wasn't into the same things, yet I stayed longer than I should have, trying to make it work, hoping it would help her trust issues.

Look where that got me.

Jumping into bed with another good girl would be repeating the same mistake.

With my luck, I'll probably run into Ellie at my aunt's next eggnog-tasting party, and she'll call me a pervert under the mistletoe.

That settles it. I'm going to walk her home, shake her hand at the door, then catch a Lyft back to my place.

Now that I'm not envisioning worst-case scenarios, I have the brain space to make small talk. As we cross the next street, I nod to her helmet. "Cute helmet."

There.

She tosses me a flirty look. "You have a thing for pink," she says.

My gaze travels down to her pink cropped top, and I'm busted. This is what happens when I try to behave. She keys in on my preference for pink.

"Pink is pretty on you," I say evenly, keeping my compliment girl-next-door appropriate and not letting on that I want to rip her clothes off. "Suits you. Nice and sweet." I don't add that the innocence of pink fries my brain and heats my skin. I have to remember she's a family friend who I'll probably see again soon.

Like at this weekend's birthday party for Ellie's aunt—my mom's bestie.

No way can I fuck Ellie tonight, then face her at a lawn party.

Playing croquet.

No thanks.

Ellie turns her gaze to me. "So, I'm nice and sweet?" It's a clear question, but maybe there's an eye roll happening too. I'm not sure in the dark. "Are you saying I'm like candy, Gabe?"

"Everyone likes candy," I say evasively, so I don't linger too long on how much like candy she is, mainly in that I want to lick her every-fucking-where.

Great. Now I'm walking with a hard-on.

New topic—stat. "The scooter lifestyle has become a thing here in the beach towns." I nod to her ride as we turn onto the next block, passing under a streetlamp. "You've taken to it quickly. Did you ride one in New York?"

She shakes her head. "Nope. I walked everywhere in New York. Or took the subway. I'm a scooter virgin. But my friend Maddox lives here in LA, and he gave it to me as a gift," she says.

I know a Maddox. Could it be the same guy? "Don't tell me your bud is Maddox LeGrande," I say. This is a big city, but I'm desperate for a topic with no pitfalls.

Her eyes widen. "That's him. How—? Oh..." She

smiles brightly. "He's a sports agent. Wait—does he rep you?"

"Nope. But he takes care of my quarterback, Drew Adams, and my buddy Carter Hendrix on the Renegades. He's sharp. One of the best in the biz."

Talking shop is keeping the tent in my pants down. I'm brilliant. I only need to steer the convo to where I can apologize for my too-forward suggestion, then somehow walk away once we reach her house.

Before I figure out how to start, though, we turn into a driveway, where Ellie opens the garage from her phone. "I need to let Gigi out real quick. Want to meet her?" She sounds so hopeful.

A good guy would say hi to her dog. "Absolutely."

I'll say hello, then jet.

Ellie shuts the garage, then opens the door to her home, and a blond blur of fur rushes at her, hopping up and down, barking enthusiastically.

The woman's face lights up. "Hello, my little lady. I know, I know. You have to go to the little girls' room," she says, baby-talking the pooch.

I cannot fuck a woman with a chihuahua. Is there any more obvious sign that Ellie's vanilla? A chihuahua is like the secret handshake of the sweet vanilla girl club.

I cannot corrupt her and then face retribution over croquet.

My mom would take me to task. My aunt would

too. They'd point out the ten-year age difference between Ellie and me. They'd remind me I used to babysit her.

The dog jumps once more, then notices me. The football-sized mutt whips around to face me, transforming into an unholy terror.

Hell, her dog will have my ass too.

"Gigi thinks she's a German shepherd." Ellie scoops up the pup and tells her, "Gabe is a friend. You can say hi to him."

Friend.

That's a gut punch. And it smarts, but hell, it's for the best. Ellie's making it clear how she sees me. Gigi must agree, since she settles down, lip uncurling, ears swiveling forward like radar dishes. I pet the pup's chin. The cutie lifts it higher, asking for more. "Ooh, you're charming her too," Ellie coos to me, then puts the dog down. Beckoning me along, Gigi heads to the back door.

Fine, one dog visit, then I am making my excuses.

Ellie slides open the back door, and while her pup races across the yard, the woman in pink slinks over to me on her deck, stopping less than a foot away, right next to an Adirondack chair. She nibbles on the corner of her lips.

A groan escapes me, unbidden, at how much I want to bite those lips too.

She's not making my great escape any easier. Everything's harder.

Then she inches closer, reaches for my shirt, tugs me toward her. "Hi. So about that question you asked me. Can we start answering it?"

Be strong.

Resist.

But when Ellie Snow stares wantonly at my mouth, my control starts to fray. One kiss, then I'll go.

One standard order kiss.

Tenderly, I pull her against me. "Can I kiss you?" I ask.

Her brow creases. Her eyes are full of question marks. "Um, yeah," she says, like *duh*.

But I have to treat her carefully for this kiss, or I'll be in a heap of trouble. So I cup her cheeks. Gently. Then I press my lips to hers and give her a barely-there smooch. I kiss slowly, stroking her cheek as I brush my lips across hers.

Take your time. Treat her with care. She won't throw rocks at you at the party, then.

But even like this, she's soft and sexy. Maybe, just maybe, I can learn to like this pace. *For her.*

Hell, with the way she smells—like cherry blossoms—and feels—like a sexy dream—I can like anything with her.

But does she even like this? She's kissing me back tentatively. Slowly, like she's testing the waters. But gradually, she takes the reins, kissing a little harder. Then Ellie rises on tiptoes and kisses me deep.

Oh, fuck. That's real nice.

I slide a hand through her hair, tenderly stroking her strands, keeping my cool when the dog who thinks she's a German Shepherd tells me off in a few sharp, stern barks.

I break the kiss. "She's trying to tell me something, I think."

Mischief glitters in Ellie's eyes. "Fortunately, I speak dog," she says, then picks up the critter. "What did you say, Gigi?"

She pretends to listen to the dog, then nods, pops the pup inside the house, and returns to me. Lifting her chin, she meets my eyes with a fearless gaze. There's been a shift from before she let the dog inside. She's ramping up to something.

"Gabe, I want you to kiss me like you'll die if you don't."

Wait. That doesn't sound like a good girl request.

"Then fuck me so hard I scream."

My world flips upside down. Are you kidding me?

But she doesn't need to ask twice. In a flash, I grip her waist, spin her around, and push her up against the wall. I devour her candy lips. In less than a second, she's squirming.

Yes, fucking yes.

I crush her mouth. Kiss her mercilessly. She moans, a scorching, seductive sound that goes straight to my balls.

I up the ante, grabbing her soft hair, wrapping the strands tightly in my fist. Then tugging hard.

She gasps, then murmurs, "Yessss."

I dip my face to her neck and bite hard enough to leave a mark.

She answers by grabbing my ass with both hands. Yanks me against her.

Yes, you do only live once.

I grin wickedly as I lick a path to her ear then nip her earlobe.

"Oh god," she whimpers, then grinds against me.

"This the surprise you wanted?" I rasp out.

"Yes. God, yes. For a while there, I thought you were going to be...really vanilla."

I laugh. We were really working at cross purposes. But I'm fucking delighted over our good luck. "And I thought you were."

"I'm not at all," she says with that same naughty list grin.

I grin. "Me neither." Then I erase the smile and stare sternly at her. "And for doubting me, you'll need to turn around right now, and raise your ass," I command.

Her eyes gleam. "Yes, sir," she taunts.

I spin her around, shove her hands up against the

smooth wood of the outside wall of her house, then smack her ass. "Did I say to call me sir?" I ask harshly.

"No, but I did it anyway," she says, the fucking vixen.

I swat her covered cheek harder.

She cries out.

My dick thumps against my jeans. That fucker is so damn happy right now. Ellie Snow is a dirty, kinky girl.

"Call me by my name only. Say it if you're aching for my dick," I tell her.

"Gabe," she groans.

"Good girl," I tell her.

Grabbing her wrists, I push her hands over her head and grind my hard-on against her ass. "You want me to spank you for lying to me?"

She turns to me, an earnest look in her eyes. "How did I lie to you?"

I brush my stubble against the smooth skin of her face. "You pretended to be good, but you're very, very bad," I hiss.

"So bad, Gabe," she pants. "Maybe you need to spank me again. Punish me."

"You need to be taught a lesson."

"Teach me, Gabe," she purrs.

I sweep her hair to the side, kiss her neck, lick a path to her jawline. She tastes so good, and my head swims with lust. "Mmm. But I think I'll make you wait for the next lesson of my hand."

"Why?" she whines.

"You need to prove you want me to fuck you hard."

She pants. "How?"

"Show me how turned on you are." I let go of her. Step back. Wait.

Slowly, she spins around, her lips parted. "Where do you want me?"

I point to the Adirondack chair. "Take off your skirt and get in that chair. Show me your pussy."

10

WHY I LIKE PINK

Gabe

Once she strips off her skirt and panties, she perches on the edge of the chair. Her breath comes in staggered gasps of anticipation.

Mine escapes in a long, guttural groan.

She's so fucking pretty.

I stare savagely at her slick, pink center. A thin landing strip leads to the paradise between her thighs. I'm so ready to feast on her, but there's one problem. Standing in front of her, stroking the hard outline of my cock, I arch a brow. "That's good, sweetheart. But there's an issue. You keep defying me."

"How?" she asks, wobbly but breathlessly.

I narrow my eyes. "I told you to *get* in the chair. Not to *sit* in it."

Her brown eyes sparkle. "How do you want me… Gabe?" There's a deliberate pause before my name as her gaze drifts down her body, inviting me to look.

She's glistening even more.

I point and draw a circle in the air. "Stand, turn around, and lift that sweet ass for me."

She obeys.

"Now, bend over, and hold on to the arms of the chair."

She complies again, and I groan at the filthy, beautiful sight. Her long, lean legs. Her creamy flesh. Her wet pussy.

I kneel behind her, cover her cheeks with my hands, and spread her apart.

She trembles.

I blow a soft stream of air against her wetness, like a promise of all the wild sensations to come. "I have one request, sweetheart," I say.

"What's that?"

"Don't want your neighbors to hear what's mine. Be fucking quiet. Or I'll spank you."

"Oh!" She wiggles her rear. "But I like spanking."

Best. Words. Ever.

But still. She's so damn impudent.

I dip my face, bite her ass. She yelps. "I said be quiet," I warn.

"But I like biting too."

"Then, if you're noisy, I won't spank you. I won't bite you," I command, and she whimpers. "Can you be quiet now?"

"I'll try."

"Good girl," I say, then I bury my face between her legs and kiss her wetness. Her salty, sweet taste floods my tongue and overwhelms my senses.

As I lick and kiss, she gasps. As I experience the forbidden thrill of eating Ellie Snow, I roam my hands across the landscape of her fantastic ass. "Want to own this ass," I mutter, then I trace a long line along her pussy, lapping her up before I return to the rise of her clit, sucking on her right there.

"Oh god," she groans.

I raise a hand and smack her rear.

She gasps quietly, then sucks in her sounds.

I smile against her. "Good."

I swat her other cheek.

She stifles a moan. So obedient.

I lick her again, smack her again. We become a feedback loop of smacks and swallowed groans, swats and strangled gasps, until Ellie white-knuckles the arms of the chair and whispers, "Gabe," in a plaintive warning.

She's on the cusp of coming, and that won't do. Can't let her lose her mind outside. I stop, stand, and toss her over my shoulder, still only half-dressed. I carry her inside, set her on the couch, and crawl between her thighs, my hands sliding up and spreading her nice and wide.

No idea where her dog is. Don't care either.

I tap her right leg. "Put this one over the side of the couch. Want to admire this pretty pussy before I fuck you with my tongue," I tell her.

With a shudder, she drapes her right leg over the cushion, letting her left leg fall to the floor. "Is this good, Gabe?"

I rumble in approval, gazing at her slippery pink lips. God, no wonder I love pink so fucking much.

Then, I French kiss her sweet cunt, worshiping her with my lips and my mouth, my hands pushing her legs open wider. She moans and writhes. But that's not enough for me. I want screams and shouts. I stretch my right arm up, push under her shirt and bra, and grab her tit.

"Yessss," she moans.

I roll her nipple between my thumb and forefinger, ruthlessly, right as I suck on her clit.

"Oh god, Gabe. *Yes. Yes. Yes.*"

I slide up my other arm. As I eat her pussy like a starving man, I squeeze her generous tits, and she arches her back.

In seconds, my Ellie is losing her mind.

Shouting my name. No. *Screaming it.* My mind

goes haywire, lights flashing, electricity crackling as she comes hard on my lips.

She tastes incredible, her scent filling my nostrils. I slow my pace, a soft, gentle lick as she comes down, panting, murmuring. When she laughs, that's a sign to stop. I lift my face, smiling wickedly at my woman. She's a blissed-out mess, hair wild, shirt rucked up, bra askew.

And we've only just begun. "Got a full-length mirror?"

Ellie smiles woozily. "Bedroom," she says in a sex-drenched voice.

"Take off your shirt. Get on the bed. If you're not on your hands and knees in ten seconds, waiting for my cock like a good girl, you'll have to wait for it while I jerk off on your face," I tell her.

She blinks, then swallows roughly. "Yes, Gabe."

She pops up and races to her bedroom, stripping on the way, dropping her tank top and bra on the floor.

I rise, tugging off my shirt. When I toss it on the couch, it lands next to...a dog.

Whoa. Was Gigi there the whole time? No clue, but this dog has excellent sex manners. "You're a good girl too," I tell the pup, then I head to the bedroom, grabbing a condom from my wallet as I reach the doorway.

Where I just stop. Awed.

It's like discovering a precious work of art. I'm overwhelmed, and I shake my head in appreciation.

She's naked and glorious on all fours. There's a mirror in front of her.

I stride over to her and drag a hand through her lush hair. "Look at me," I command.

She raises her face. "Yes?"

"You like this? You like the way I fuck you?"

She nods, whip fast. "You haven't fucked me yet."

I yank, punitively, on her hair. "Everything I do to you is fucking, sweetheart. Got that? When I eat your pussy, I'm fucking you with my tongue. When I finger you, I fuck you with my fingers. Every way we touch, we fuck."

She trembles, a long, luxurious shudder that moves down her beautiful back. "I love the way you fuck me."

"Are you dripping for me?"

"Yes," she says.

"Prove it. Now," I order.

She slips a hand between her thighs. When she shows me her wet fingers, I rub my free hand over my cock. "Put it on your lips, so I can taste you again," I say.

She runs her fingertip over her lower lip, like she's applying lip gloss. I bend and lick off the tang of her. My brain nearly short-circuits with lust.

I break the kiss and focus on brass tacks.

"Pick a safe word," I tell her.

Her lips curve in a grin of filthy delight. "Scooter."

I smile too. "Perfect, sweetheart," I tell her, then I strip off my jeans and boxer briefs, move to the other side of the bed, and climb behind her, kneeling between her spread thighs again.

"Now watch in the mirror. Don't want you to have any doubts about whether I'd give you vanilla sex or not," I instruct, then roll a condom down my length and notch the head of my cock against her slick heat.

And I sink inside.

Then go still.

I need a moment as her body hugs my cock. She's tight and hot and fits me like a glove. "This pussy belongs to me," I growl as I push all the way inside her.

"I know," she pants, her head falling forward.

My disobedient Ellie. No, no, no. I grab her shoulder. "Watch us," I warn. "Or I'll stop."

She blinks like she's orienting herself, remembering her orders. "Yes, Gabe," she says as she raises her face and gazes at us in the mirror.

Then I curl my hand tighter around her shoulder, my fingers digging in possessively. I ease out almost, *almost* all the way.

She moans. Her back bows and she lifts her ass, inviting me to slam into her.

I heed her wishes. Thrusting deep inside her. Gripping her harder. Listening to her cues, reading her body language, I find our rhythm, a punishing pace that makes her groan and grunt too. We're both animals, fucking wildly.

I shove a hand into her hair again. Twist her strands around my fist. Jerk hard.

The sound she makes is feral. "Ohhhh," she moans.

And it's still not enough for me. "You want me to smack this pretty ass?"

"Hard, please," she begs.

I lift a hand, then smack.

Smack, tug, fuck.

I leave handprints, and still she's begging me, *more, more, more.*

She cries out again, like she's closer, and I let go of her hair. Sliding my hand between her thighs, I stroke her diamond of a clit and I smack her ass ruthlessly with my other hand until she's shouting my name and coming on my cock.

My vision blurs.

My brain goes offline as my climax seizes my cells. Pleasure obliterates everything but white-hot bliss with this woman who wants the same kind of wild, dirty, kinky, uninhibited sex I do.

I've never been so glad to be wrong about someone.

Sated, for now, I lie next to her and give her the sweet, tender kiss she deserves.

"You took that fucking so well," I tell her, then brush a gentle kiss to her lips.

"You fucked me so well," she whispers.

I wrap her in my arms, hold her close, and stroke her hair. "Can I stay the night?"

She smiles against me. "You better."

We lie together in satisfied silence, and I lazily take in the details of her bedroom. On the nightstand is a stack of books—romance novels with titles like *Sweet Spot, Top-Notch Boyfriend,* and *Come Lately.*

I point to the books. "Those look good," I say, then I read the spine of another one. *Role Play.*

"They're unputdownable." She nods to the last one. "And they sometimes give me great ideas."

Milo was right. There is something sexy about a reader. But when her hand brushes mine as she reaches for the book, there's something...surprisingly *nice* about it too.

Like reading could be another thing to do in bed.

I try to knock away the thought of other bedroom activities. But as she starts chapter one, the idea stays.

11

GABE COCKTAIL

Ellie

We lounge around until hunger drives us out of bed and in search of sustenance. Feeling famished, I pop the cork on a Riesling while Gabe answers the door for the food delivery.

I pulled on a comfy T-shirt and shorts post-sex. Gabe is shirtless, and the view from the kitchen counter is quite nice.

What is it about the whole jeans, bare feet, and nothing else look that does it for me?

Silly question, Ellie.

Gabe could be wearing pantaloons and I'd salivate. I don't take my eyes off him as I pour a glass, watching him reach for the bag of Thai food with his ink-covered arm.

"Thanks for the delivery," he says to the Ding and Dine driver. "Appreciate everything you do."

"Anytime. And, hey, have a good training camp. Glad they traded you here," the guy says.

"Me too. Especially lately," he replies.

Lately, huh? Is that lately, as in the last few hours? I hope so.

"What do you think about the team's chances this year?" the driver asks.

"I always play like we're going to the Super Bowl." Gabe's friendly answer is positive but not over-confident.

"Have you got your hacky sacks?" the driver asks and Gabe nods.

I smile. Definitely a fan if he knows Gabe's game rituals, like how when the Mercenaries are on a winning streak, he plays hacky sack on the sidelines.

"Here's hoping you'll be playing hacky sack *a lot*," the driver says.

"I hope so too." With his free hand, Gabe knocks fists with the guy then shuts the door and joins me in the kitchen, unpacking our food at the counter.

"You're quite the charmer with bartenders and delivery guys," I remark as I waggle the Riesling bottle in question. "Wine? Or are you a bourbon-or-bust guy?"

"I'm not picky about food, liquor, or music," he says, then drops his voice. "Only sex."

A shiver runs over my shoulders. "Good answer," I say, then pour and slide him a glass.

"And why wouldn't I be nice to delivery guys and bartenders? Or anyone else, for that matter?"

I shrug as I open the carton of papaya salad. "I agree, but I've known guys who were jerks to servers and such."

Gabe scowls as he parks himself on the stool next to mine. "What's up with people who are dicks to service workers?"

I take a sip. "I'm just glad you're a friendly guy," I say, then grab my chopsticks and dig in.

"I don't know any other way to be. My parents are like that. Guess it rubbed off on me."

"Your parents are the cutest. They were adorable at their anniversary party. Forty years and still in love," I say, a little warm and fuzzy from the memory.

"Yeah, they're goals for sure. They always have been," he says.

A guy who truly likes his parents? Who admires their marriage? I cannot get hooked on Gabe. Luckily this is just a sex thing.

I snag a forkful of the salad. "Want some? Since you're not picky."

He moves closer, parts his lips, and waits. I feed him some papaya, and yes, Gabe eats it sensually.

That's just his way.

"Mmm. That's tasty. Not the best thing I've eaten tonight, but close," he says with a sly smile.

"Glad to hear it's your second favorite."

As he twirls some of his drunken noodles around his chopsticks, he tips his forehead to my carton and asks, "Are you vegetarian?"

"I am, and I'm heading down the Vegan Brick Road now too," I say.

He laughs. "That's cool. Why'd you make that decision?"

"Gigi."

His brow knits. "Is she vegan?"

"Oh god, no. But I just love animals so much I can't eat them. It's not a hardship either. Confession: I love salad madly. I swear it's not the actress stereotype. I just seriously love salad so much I could marry it."

He tips his wine glass to mine. "To the future Mrs. Arugula," he says.

"You should know I'm going into a polyamorous relationship with kale, arugula, and spinach. Not radicchio, though. A gal's got to have standards."

"I'll revise my earlier statement to exclude radicchio. I like everything but radicchio. That's an unforgivable leaf."

"I couldn't agree more."

As he takes another bite, he tilts his head, a

thoughtful look in his eyes. "Do you want me to eat vegan when we're together?"

Wow. No one has ever asked me that before. "That's very considerate to ask, but it's a personal choice. Thank you, though."

"Just let me know if you change your mind, Ellie," he says.

Gabe's an interesting mix of gentlemanly consideration outside the bedroom and caveman in it.

I do like this cocktail of Gabe.

"I'll let you know." I take another bite of the salad before I go fishing. "So, you told the driver you're liking LA?"

He grins. "Even more in the last few hours," he says.

I smile and happily tuck that compliment in my pocket. "Me too."

We take a few more bites, then he says, "Tell me more about your show. When I looked you up, I read a little about *The Dating Games*. Two best friends, a man and a woman. The guy's gay, the woman's straight. And they give each other dating challenges? How'd you come up with that concept?"

This is new. A guy who asks questions and wants to know the me behind the face he might have seen on-screen. "The thing I loved most about acting was inventing the backstories for characters, so while I was working on *Unfinished Business,* I started playing around with the concept for *The Dating Games*. It comes from situations I saw around me—things my friends and I experienced. Dating these days is such a minefield," I say.

"Sure is," he seconds.

"I wanted to tell a fun, fresh, sometimes poignant story that reflected the highs and lows for these two friends. Both are coming off breakups and getting back into the dating world by giving each other bets and challenges."

"It's as much about friendship as it is about romance?"

"Yes! Exactly. At its heart, it's about how we lean on our friends as we seek romance," I say. "I know I wouldn't be able to get through the crazy world of dating without my friends."

"Will you miss them while you're in LA?"

"So much." I set a hand on my heart, feeling that pang of missing Veronica and Hazel even though they're still here this week. "But I plan on making great new friendships in Los Angeles. It's my top goal after work."

He smiles. "Love that plan." Then he clears his expression and takes another bite. When he's done chewing, his gaze is intense and so is his tone. "No interest in dating?"

Well, I didn't plan on it, but tonight was fun.

I don't say that, though, since I can't quite read why he's asking with such...passion?

He clearly cares about the answer, so I mull over his question for a few seconds. Originally, I thought I might date when I first arrived. But I'll be working relentless hours starting next week, building a new name for myself in the entertainment business.

Even though dating a sexy beast like Gabe might be fun, I'm here for one reason only, and I need to focus on my new work opportunity. "I wasn't planning on it," I say at last, feeling solid about that answer. "Work is going to be intense, and it's a big change. So is setting up my life here. Making new friends," I add with a knowing smile, bumping my shoulder to his. He's been a friend of sorts. He could surely stay one beyond whatever tonight is.

"New friends," he says, like he's taking everything in. He blows out a long, relaxed breath. "Makes perfect sense. I'm all about football. That should be intense too. Always is but especially since this is my last season."

I nod slowly as I shift through what he's telling me. "And you want to give it your all," I venture.

"Absolutely," he says crisply. "I don't want distractions. Just like you with your new gig."

I feel tentatively for the boundary of what we could be. Gabe is decisive. That must be why he asked the *any interest in dating* question with such intensity—because he wanted to be certain I wasn't interested in a relationship. And decisive is a good thing when laying out rules for...whatever we seem to be setting limits on.

Whether we're a one-night thing. Or maybe two nights? How many would I even want?

But when I stare down at my schedule, the answer seems pretty easy—the next few nights until I start the new job. Plus, I don't want to take any more chances. "And honestly, I've had some bad relationships," I admit.

"Same here, Ellie." He knocks back some wine as he studies my face. "That's why you took the good guy challenge? Because you've had some bad dates?"

"I did." It's so much easier to talk to him now than it was at the start of the date. When I met him at the bar, I wasn't completely honest. Now we've revealed our desires, so maybe that's why it's easier to share. "I'm trying to be more careful. Read the situation better and all."

"I'm trying to do the same," he says, then shrugs resignedly. "Except I don't know if I've improved. I pegged you for a princess who'd kick me out for wanting dirty sex."

I scoff. "What about me gives off the goody-two-shoes vibe?"

He gestures to Gigi's red velvet throne. "Your cute

dog." Then to me, with a playful smile. "Your cute jeans. Your cute clothes. Your cute self."

I poke his chest. "My naughty texts. My sexy clothes. My yes to your *can I take you home and fuck you.*"

He clears his throat. "Ahem. And your self-proclaimed good guy challenge. *That* made me think you wanted sweet, butterfly kisses and soft lovemaking," he teases.

Touché. "Fine. You win that round," I say with a laugh.

"Good. I like winning." He goes thoughtful for a moment, his gaze turned inward like he's turning something over in his head. I wait, curious as to what he'll say, and when he's ready, there's a gleam in his eyes. "If you like dating challenges so much, I have one for you."

I'm intrigued, in a good way, and I lean forward. "Hit me up."

"I don't want this to be a one-night stand. I need more of your mouth. Your pussy. Your sweet, beautiful tits," he says.

Hello, five-alarm fire! This man can go from zero to sixty in the dirty department. I'm determined to keep up. "And I want more of your cock. Your mouth. Your hands."

He lets out a dirty rumble. "Your production starts next week. My training camp starts then too.

We have a big team meeting on Sunday, then on Monday, I take off for San Diego. How about we do this for the rest of the week?"

The suggestion is deliciously straightforward and clear. It also answers all my questions about rules. We now know what *this* is—a brief but scorching-hot fling. And what it isn't—*anything serious*. He leaves town next week. I hunker down then for the show. We both need laser focus on our jobs.

It's a relief that I'm on all the same pages as Gabe, but I tease him about the one thing I can. "What's *this* exactly?"

He leans in to brush his knuckles along my cheek. "*This* is you screaming my name as I find new ways to fuck you every night," he says.

A fog of lust wraps around me, and I give the only possible answer. "Yes."

He shifts back in his stool, looking terribly pleased. "Good. Then, we'll do *this* for the week, and you'll be my date at your aunt Tilly's big birthday party on Saturday."

I smack his shoulder playfully. "Shut up!"

"Ouch," he says, wincing playfully as he rubs his shoulder.

"Gabe! I was going to ask you to go with me. My mom is threatening to set me up with other guys from our hometown."

He narrows his eyes. "Nope," he says in a stern command.

"Nope what?"

His brown eyes darken. "You're not going with someone else from our hometown."

"I'm not?" I ask, feigning innocence.

"No fucking way," he says.

"Why not?"

"You're not going with someone from an app. You're not going with someone from your show. You're not going with some other guy. Case closed," he says, then moves off the stool and wraps those strong arms tight about my waist. "You're mine this week. You go with me. Only with me. I don't want any other man even looking at what's mine."

What's mine.

I ache from this possession. "I'm yours this week," I murmur.

"You fucking are, Ellie. Mine, only mine. And I will treat you that way." He slides a hand down my throat, over my chest, then squeezes my right breast. "Don't want another man thinking he can have you."

But Gabe can't have me either. He's not available, nor am I. We might be screwing, but we're not truly dating, so it's best to put all our cards on the table. "So, I'm like a one-week girlfriend?"

He seems to think about that, then says thoughtfully, "A fake real girlfriend." Then he adds, "How's that for a dating challenge?"

I smile. "Perfect." But I want to be clear on what this means, so I ask, "At the party, we're sort of pretending we're together?"

He tilts his head. "The party where our book club moms will be serving apple pie and lemonade? Where our dads will be making barbecue? Playing lawn croquet? No, we're not pretending we're together." He lets go of my breast so he can wrap a big hand around my ass, then he smacks my cheek, and I shudder. "We're pretending we're wholesome," he corrects as he swats the other.

I gasp. "Can we practice being wholesome this week in public?"

He dips his face to kiss my neck. "We need all the practice we can get. So we're gonna date publicly like we're good, and privately I'm going to fuck you senseless," he says as he kisses me.

My breath catches in excitement. "I'm a very good actress."

"You are. But you'll never need to act in bed with me. In fact, we're going to practice coming in a few minutes. This time you'll be crying out my name while you're sitting on my face."

I'm ready to ride him into the night. But I do want one more thing from him. "Gabe?" I ask coyly, twirling my hair. "There's something I want too."

"Name it," he says, retaking his dominant tone. "And I'll see if you deserve it."

I bat my lashes. "That thing you promised me earlier if I didn't make it to bed on time."

The facial.

His smile is filthy as he strokes my cheek, then runs his thumb over my mouth. "You want that, sweetheart?"

Breathlessly, I say, "I do."

"Then you'll get it. But *only* after you fuck my face. So, go," he says, waving me off. "I'll clean up the kitchen. You get naked. When I walk into the bedroom in a couple of minutes, I want to find you with your legs spread wide and you playing with your pussy, getting yourself nice and hot and wet for me. You better be fucking yourself when I find you in there."

"I promise," I say, and I race to the bedroom.

WEDNESDAY

A Nice Day for a Stroll along the Greens

12

A BOX FOR YOUR BOX

Ellie

The bright Los Angeles morning streams through the window and wakes me up.

That's weird. Usually Gigi wakes me up with her tongue on my face.

Dog kisses are a sign she needs to go out. Where is my little lover?

I blink my eyes open. Gigi's nibbling on a stuffed giraffe at the foot of the bed. She's wearing her black harness with skulls on it. Well, she's a smarty pants, but with no thumbs, she can't dress herself.

"Did Gabe take you for a walk, girl?"

She growls around the giraffe's neck, then shakes it again.

But there's no sign of Gabe. The pillow's fluffed and his side of the mattress is empty. I push up on my elbows.

I swing my legs over the edge of the bed, then head to the living room. No shoes, no phone, no man.

In the kitchen, I find a sheet of paper on the counter. It's from a notebook Veronica gave me that says *to-do list*.

Dear Ellie,

I took the liberty to work on a to-do list. How's this?

—Practice for the lawn croquet appearance.

—Wear seersucker shorts to play the part? A flower dress for you. With a bonnet?

— Bake a cherry pie?

In other news, I took Gigi for a walk this morning. She was kissing my face, and I took that to mean she had to pee. Guess I'm learning dog language. I have to take off for a morning run with Drew and Carter.

By the way, since I was so bad when I fucked you on the

first date, tonight we can role-play being good. Like how they did in that scene you read to me last night.

Incidentally, you reading in bed, squirming over the spicy parts, gets me hard.

You've been warned.

If you're up for it, meet me at six.

See? Six is too early for sex.

Gabe, the good guy

I read it a few more times, smiling. No time is too early for sex. I grab my phone to reply. ***Tell me where to be at this supposedly sexless hour of the day.***

He shoots me an address, and when I Google it, I laugh, then write back. ***I'll be there, and thanks for walking my girl.***

Then I shower and do my best to put thoughts of Gabe aside as I head to my Webflix meeting. When I meet with the execs, I can't spend my time lingering on how deliciously sore I am, or how much I like that he took care of my dog.

I go into the meeting like a badass boss lady in charge of a new TV show.

After my morning meeting, I head to a lunch spot in Venice. Veronica's Date Night for One party will be held on the back patio of a trendy sandwich joint this afternoon. Sexy sunshine music drifts from the shop, and I head to the back to help my friend set up.

I don't see Veronica, but I spot Hazel at a long white table, tying a bow on a box of toys. I rush up behind her to pinch her butt.

"Ooh baby," she says, then turns to shoot me a knowing look. "I knew it was you."

"I should hope so. And by the way, your idea was brilliant. The challenge date."

She beams. "Sometimes we just need a change in our lives."

"Cool. You'll move to LA then?" I ask, with a too-big smile.

Hazel scans the patio like she's making sure no one can hear. But it's only us. "Actually, I'm going to Europe soon," she confesses.

My jaw drops. "To move?"

"Maybe for a little bit. My next novel is set in Europe, and I want to do some research there," she says.

"That sounds awful," I say. "So awful I may need to stow away in your luggage."

"Please. You'll be busy here conquering another industry," she says, then shakes a finger at me. "But stop distracting me. How good was the date?"

"So good. I'm going to see him again...*tonight,*" I say, a little thrilled to share.

Hazel blows on her nails. "I'm taking the credit. Since I gave you that challenge."

"And you deserve it." Then I shrug happily. "I'll probably see him a few more times this week."

She jerks her gaze back. "So, you really like him?" Her question turns a touch serious.

But quickly, I dismiss the gravitas vibes. "We're hanging out this week only. We both have a ton going on next week when he starts training camp and I start the show. So we're just having fun for a couple days."

She seems to chew on that for a few seconds, then says, "Then have the most fun of all."

"Oh, I plan to," I say, then pull her away from the table toward the back of the patio for more privacy. "Do you think boss ladies like to be dominated in the bedroom?"

"So it was *that* good," she says with a laugh. Then her eyes turn thoughtful. "Some do."

"It's a bit wild how much I love being in charge of my destiny at work and how little control I want in bed." I'm not surprised I liked sleeping with Gabe. I'm surprised at how much I liked the kind of sex we had. "I've always liked sex a little rough. A little hard. But Gabe is next level in the bedroom. He's an animal," I confess, shivers running down my spine as images of him flash before me. "And I loved it."

"Loved what?"

At Veronica's question, I spin around. Sporting a yellow sundress, she saunters across the patio. With her is a pretty brunette in skinny jeans and a tank, with a boho tangle of necklaces draped across her throat. That must be Veronica's client who owns the jewelry shop. "This is Rachel Dumont," Veronica says of the fashionable woman next to her. "And she wanted to throw the party for her friends, customers, and fellow business owners."

Rachel gestures to the party-size table full of white boxes with pink bows. "Because every woman needs a box for her box."

It's official. I'm in love with Rachel. I stride over to the new kid on the friend block. "I'm Ellie. We're going to become new besties. I've just decided it."

"Sounds like a plan," Rachel says.

And I have a plan too, for my date tonight. In a few more hours, I'll be pretending to be good.

13

THAT'S A NEW MINI GOLF STRATEGY

Ellie

If I'd known dating with a built-in boundary would be so freeing, I'd have done it sooner.

As I wait for Gabe outside the mini golf rental counter, the usual *will this turn into something* worries are all gone. In their place is just...excitement over tonight.

This is how dating should be.

At six on the dot, Gabe strolls across the parking lot, looking like he belongs at a country club.

Yes. I like his costume.

Tonight, he's a perfect prepster, striding up to me wearing khakis and a sky-blue polo.

When he stops a few feet away, I grin in delight at

the pièce de résistance—the tiny tennis racket icon stitched onto the shirt. He understood the assignment—play the part.

I smooth a hand over his collar. "You are *so* the boy next door," I say.

He doesn't answer. Instead, his brown eyes travel up and down my body. He smirks as he takes in my pink dress with white polka dots. The good-girl costume comes complete with a pink headband. I even curled the ends of my hair for the full-on sexy retro housewife look.

With an appreciative sigh, he loops his inked arm around my waist. "And your girl-next-door skirt is perfect for spanking you," he whispers.

I tsk at him, wagging a finger. "Gabe, you have to behave," I chide.

He narrows his eyes. Rubs his stubbled jaw against my cheek. "Whose ridiculous idea was that?"

"Yours," I say, laughing. "You said we needed to practice being good."

His fingers go exploring, taking a trip over my rear. He squeezes, rumbling out, "I know what I want to practice."

"Patience," I warn. "You can't keep tempting me."

He kisses my neck. "The fuck I can't," he whispers.

"Mmm. You're trying to get me to give in on a golf

course," I murmur. "You want me to be the one to break character."

"So I can have you on a golf course? Works for me," he says, then explores the terrain of my neck, kissing up to my ear. "I want to see you give in to me. Want you to break first and say *take me home now*."

God, I feel like I'm ready to say that right this second.

But we can't just jump into the sack. We made a deal to go to a party and behave. "Soon, soon," I say.

With a huff, he lets go of me, then shakes his head like he's resetting. He drags his hand through his thick, wavy hair, a little unkempt. The wild side of him can't be fully tamed with clothes, and I love that the ink and messy hair are a peek into who he truly is—a little wild, a little dangerous around the edges.

He licks his lips. "Let's play a game. Whoever gets the other to break first can pick the fantasy we'll act out tonight."

A hot spark sizzles down my chest. "I've never done role play before," I confess quietly as a pack of teenage girls in midriff-baring tops rushes past us to the course.

"Me neither," he says quietly, his eyes glimmering.

"But I want to," I say, electrified already by the possibilities. Role play and I seem like a perfect fit.

"So do I," he says, excited too.

"Then you're on," I say, offering a hand to shake.

Instead, he presses a kiss to the top of my hand. Then, he links his fingers through mine. As we walk toward the entrance, he looks down at our joined hands then drops a chaste kiss onto my cheek. "But holding hands with you is pretty nice too."

I try to fight off a big grin, but it's futile. "Sure is," I say.

Hand-in-hand, in costume, we walk into the clubhouse.

After he pays for the game, we pick up clubs, balls, and a scorecard, and we head to the first hole where a windmill sweeps in circles.

He takes a few practice swings as I set my purple ball on a tee. "How was your day?"

For a second, I wonder if he's trying to knock me off my golf game with small talk. So he can choose the fantasy. But the question comes out honestly. Curiously.

"It was excellent. I went to a sex-toy afternoon tea," I say, faux primly.

He blinks. "I'm going to need to hear all about that," he says.

"Well, let me just play this hole, and then I'll tell you all about the latest in the world of pleasure," I say.

"I think you're trying to break me, Ellie Snow," he says.

I give him a coy shrug. "Of course I am, Gabe," I say, then nibble on the corner of my glossy lips.

My eyes drift down to his slacks, where a ridge tents the fabric.

Yup.

My strategy is working.

Then I tap the ball and send it...right into the windmill. Damn. I stomp my foot in frustration. "I'm terrible at golf," I whine.

He laughs and takes his turn. He knocks in the red ball in two putts. This tracks. Football players often love their golf.

I finish in six swings.

As we walk to the next hole, he says, "So, the tea. Tell me more about it."

"For real?"

He gives me a look like he couldn't possibly be asking any other way. "Yes, for real. I want to hear about it."

This is surprisingly nice. Talking about my day, that is. Dexter never wanted to know.

"My friend Veronica started a sex-toy subscription box," I say. Then I catch him up to speed with Date Night for One. "And she has clients all over the country now. She's done so well."

"She's an entrepreneur. That's fantastic," Gabe

says. I'm so happy that he sees that—and that he said it. How many guys would have gone for the easy joke about her peddling sex toys?

"She is," I agree. "After some complications at her last job, she had to reinvent herself, but it turned into something that makes her happy."

"We should all aspire to find some happiness in what we do. From what you were telling me last night about your show, it sounds like you feel that way about your job too?"

"I do," I say as we round a bend in the course toward the next hole. "I'm guessing it's the same for you?"

"Absolutely. Every goddam game I play. It's such a rush." But he doesn't say more about football, instead turning the talk back to me. "I know you miss your friends."

My heart squeezes. "So much. But I've already made a brand-new friend in LA," I say, then I tell him about Rachel as we take turns on the course. "What about you? You've been traded a bunch of times. You were in Miami, in Las Vegas, in Seattle. Was it hard to go to so many teams?"

Then I wince. Is that a sore spot?

"I guess nobody wants to keep me," he says, with an exaggerated frown.

I bump my shoulder against his firm arm, relieved he took it lightly. "Please. I think it's because everybody in the league wants you," I say, upbeat. I hope he sees it that way too. "I'm no football expert, but I think it shows you're versatile and can fit into any team. And that you can handle anything thrown at you."

He winks. "Pun intended." Then his expression turns thoughtful for a beat. "I don't mind that I'm not a Pioneer or a Wolf for life," he says, naming the Vegas and Seattle mascots as examples. "They've all been good trades. I can't really complain. Especially since Miami was good to me."

I glance at his hand. I know he won a ring playing for Miami, but this is the first he's brought it up.

"Why don't you wear your ring? That would be fun to show off. Lord knows I'd be flashing it at everyone if I had one."

He shrugs like he hasn't given the topic much thought. "Jewelry's not my thing. But nobody can ever take it away from me," he says, then he lines up and taps the ball straight under a tyrannosaurus rex.

I whistle. "You are damn good at this," I say.

He stops to press a possessive kiss to my lips. "A lot of years in the NFL, sweetheart. I've played a lot of golf," he says.

"Cocky," I tease.

He squeezes my ass. "And you like it."

I like just about everything about him. And I

need to just enjoy his company and this beautiful LA evening, and let next week be next week. But I don't want to linger on that thought. Or what liking him might mean after this week of fun and games ends.

A few holes later, I'm at the tee of another hole, peering down the grassy hill, sizing up whether I can send the purple ball over or around a tiny bridge, when warm breath floats past my ear. "Let me help you, sweetheart," he rasps out.

Before I can protest, Gabe lines his big body behind mine, his chest pressing against my back, his pelvis against my ass. Then his hands come down around mine on the club. "Did I ask for help?"

"No, but I'm doing it anyway," he says, then brushes his lips along my neck. Tingles slide over my skin.

"Why is that?" I murmur as pleasure zips over me.

"I thought that would be obvious," he says in a dirty rasp. "I want you to break first, Ellie."

His words make me ache. But I try hard to stay in the moment and in the game. "Why do you want me to give in, Gabe?"

He nips on my earlobe. "Because I've been staring at you in that skirt for far too long," he says, then tugs me tighter against him.

Moaning in my ear.

Are there other people nearby? Don't know, don't

care right now. I rub against his erection. "Maybe I want to break you down," I whisper.

Gabe slides a hand down the front of my skirt to the hem, playing with the fabric. "Sweetheart, *I know* you want to be broken. You want to be stretched across my lap, lifting that skirt for me, showing me that sweet ass."

So much.

My breath hitches. But I try to keep playing our game. I try to break him, to goad him into giving in. "And what makes you think that?"

"Because I've been working on a certain fantasy this whole game," he says in a low, smoky voice that makes me shiver.

"You have?" I ask.

He kisses down my neck again, telling me his fantasy.

And I call it quits on the golf game. "Let's go now. You win."

Let the bedroom games begin.

14

———

CAUGHT IN THE ACT

Ellie

I'm curled up on my couch, my hair in pigtails, a white shirt tied right under my breasts, a short plaid skirt showing off most of my legs.

Gigi's sitting by my side as I scroll aimlessly on a tablet, paying no heed to what's on the screen.

I'm *only* interested in what—or, more accurately, *who's*—coming through the door any second. When I hear the sound of the lock opening, my thighs clench. I don't look up from the couch. Giddy with anticipation, I stay focused squarely on the screen as the door swings open. Gigi lifts her head and tilts it. But she doesn't break character either. Nor do I when

I finally look up, gasp theatrically, and say, "Oh no! Mr. Clements is home early from the PTA meeting."

Footsteps grow louder. Gabe comes into the living room, staring at me.

Quickly, I slam the tablet case shut. Caught in the act. "I wasn't expecting to see you so soon," I say, playing up the breathless surprise.

He steps closer, eyeing me suspiciously. "What were you doing, Ellie?"

"Oh nothing, nothing at all," I say, twirling one of my pigtails innocently.

He arches a doubtful brow as he strides toward me, pointing to the evidence on the table. "Looks like you were doing something with my tablet."

I scramble to answer the accusation. "I had to look up something for my Math 101 homework. But the baby's sound asleep. Everything is fine. There's nothing for you to worry about, Mr. Clements. I can just straighten up and go home to my parents."

"You'll do nothing of the sort," he growls. Stalks over to me. Stands in front of me with arms crossed, giving me a clear sense of his height and breadth. "I heard moans from the screen. That didn't sound like your freshman math class at university. Sounds more triple-X rated, Ellie," he says, so stern that sparks race down my chest.

"Please don't be mad at me, Mr. Clements." I

gulp, leaning into the role. "I swear I don't know what you heard."

He reaches a hand down and grabs my chin. "I heard the babysitter watching porn on my tablet," he bites out.

My lower lip quivers. "I'm so sorry."

He runs his thumb roughly along my jawline. "For lying or watching my videos?"

My lips twitch. I drop the contrition. Jut up a shoulder. "I wanted to know what you liked," I admit in a naughty whisper. "I've been thinking about it every time you've had me babysit."

I glance at his pants and his cock tenting those khakis. He's as turned on by our games as I am. I can't wait to play more. To see how far we can go. To try all these things I've never done.

"And what do I like?" Gabe asks, moving to stand between my legs, pushing my knees wider, spreading my thighs open.

I smile coyly. "You like Daddy-does-the-babysitter porn," I say sweetly.

His expression is mean. His eyes full of punishment. "And you aren't supposed to know. So you know what that means?"

"You're going to teach me a lesson?"

"Damn right I am," he says, and in a flash, he's parked on the couch, jerking me across his lap.

I raise my ass for him. "Teach me a lesson, Mr. Clements," I coo.

He pushes up the short skirt all the way to my waist. His breath catches, telling me he wasn't expecting me to go commando.

But he stays in the role as he reaches across my ass, grabbing the tablet on the table. Like we planned. Without warning, he thwacks it sharply across the back of my thighs. I twitch. Then draw a tight, excited breath. "But I was so bad. Do you need to spank me again?"

"You're such a naughty girl, Ellie," he hisses. "You need to learn not to look at my porn."

This time, he swats my ass. A hot burst of pain rushes along my flesh, radiating into pleasure. "I don't think I've learned it yet, Daddy," I say.

Another smack. Another sweet ache between my thighs. Then he sets the tablet down. Runs his palm along one bare cheek, then the other. "You're not wearing any panties," he says, stating the obvious.

I look up at him from my prone position, giving a *who me* look.

"Why the fuck is that?" he demands. "And you better tell me the truth."

My breath comes out in a staggered gasp. "I was playing with myself before you came in. When I was watching your bookmarked videos," I confess.

A filthy rumble works its way up his chest, and he

lifts a hand high. Brings it down hard. I yelp and then I gush between my thighs as a gorgeous mix of pleasure and pain bursts under my skin. For a second, maybe more, he breaks character. "Fuck, baby, you're so hot," he murmurs. "You're such a pretty, dirty girl."

The praise lights me up. That's new too—the pleasure of being praised in bed.

Then he turns me on higher and hotter when he adds, "You're *my* dirty girl. Mine, just mine. All mine."

Instantly, I'm wetter. Achy between my thighs.

Then, it is on.

Smack, strike, tingle.

Over and over he whacks me with his palm as I wriggle and beg for it.

Gabe slides a hand between my thighs, groaning ravenously when he feels how slippery I am. "Mmm. You're ready now. You know what I like. You saw it on the video. Do it," he commands.

With my ass bruised and tingling, I scramble off him, get on the floor. Look up with eager eyes. "You want me to suck your cock like a good girl?"

He slides a hand over my head and tugs hard on one pigtail. "That's right. Take me deep and gag on my dick," he says.

I open wide, waiting patiently for my reward as he undoes the button of his slacks, then the zipper, then pushes down his pants. His boxer briefs go next. I gasp when I see his gorgeous, throbbing cock.

A drop of arousal pearls the head. "Look what you did to me." He grunts, his eyes like slits as he runs a hand along his cock then over that tempting drop of liquid.

I raise my chin, waiting.

He slides the arousal across my top lip. Then my bottom lip. Then leans closer. "Now, do a good fucking job and I'll hire you again. Do it just like you saw when you were checking out my porn," he says.

I am on fire. Pretty sure he is too. I've never had sex like this. This wild, this risqué, this...*fun.*

And I'm hungry for more of it. Tonight, tomorrow, and the next day too.

Right now, though, I want to show him how deeply I crave him.

As I take him down my throat, swirling my tongue along his length, desire throbs tightly in my core.

He's at my mercy now and I take my turn at making him lose control, giving him a deep, enthusiastic blow job with loud, long slurps that seem to excite him more. Every noise I make earns me a groan, then a grunt.

I'm scorched, my skin sizzling everywhere.

I'm rocking my hips, fucking air. I slide a hand between my thighs, stroking myself as I go. The deeper I take him, the more he shakes and shudders. His thrusts grow wilder, faster. His moans louder. "Fuck, Ellie, baby," he says, his voice strangled. "Play with my balls." He sounds like he's begging.

I fondle them, rolling them.

He shoves his cock deeper.

I gag, but I don't want him to stop, and he knows it. I told him in advance to keep going, and I keep sucking voraciously.

Then, I wet my fingers one more time with my own juices. Right when he's muttering my name and groaning so loudly I'm sure my neighbors will hear, I slide a damp finger below his balls, pressing it against his ass, then up.

He sings like a chorus of heavenly orgasm angels are flying inside him. "Oh god, oh fuck. Yes, yes, yes."

With a wickedly satisfied grin, I drink him down. He's salty and musky, and I love it.

When I drop him from my mouth, he's panting savagely for a while. Then, he recovers, pats his thighs. "Get up here on my lap and straddle me."

In a flurry, I climb onto his thighs, my legs spread. I'm so close already, and I'm dying for release.

The second he touches me, I'm riding the pleasure of his fingers till I'm shooting to the sky.

Then we're kissing like mad, hungry beasts.

I feel that way with him and it's...freeing.

It's thrilling.

It's everything I didn't know I needed in bed.

Then, this connection becomes even more when we slow down, coasting into a slow, tender, sensual kiss. Somehow, the dirty games make the gentle moments more poignant, more powerful. His mouth never leaves mine. He cups my cheeks and bestows beautiful, slow-burn kisses all over my lips.

It feels like he's claiming me.

Like every way he touches me—hard and rough, soft and gentle—is a mark. He's marking me as his.

That's a crazy thought. I can't be his after two nights of uninhibited sex.

I just can't.

But I can enjoy it for tonight.

When he breaks the kiss, he strokes a hand down my bare arm. "That'll teach you to look at my porn."

I smile, feeling woozy and wonderful. "It'll teach me to do it again and again."

Gabe wraps his hands through my messy pigtails and kisses me softly one more time. "Good. I want it again and again. Want *you* again."

And I want to make the most of the few nights we have. "Then you should have me all night long," I say, snuggling up against him. I sigh contentedly. "I need to get my fill of you this week."

He smiles against my hair, kisses me. "I'll fill you up the next few nights, sweetheart."

I laugh, then he holds me tighter. It feels good to cozy up with him like this. I'll miss it when it's gone.

But I don't tell him that. Because, really, I won't have time to miss him.

Besides, I'm enjoying this week with him like I would a rich, decadent dessert I can have only rarely—I'm devouring every bite.

Next week is back to salad and quinoa, and hey, I need that kind of fuel for work.

It's a good thing we laid out the rules in advance. That way I won't even be tempted to take another bite. A brand-new romance wouldn't survive our demanding lives anyway.

Yes, I like dating with boundaries very much.

THURSDAY

A Day for Telephone Tag

15

———

THE MORNING AFTER

Gabe

In the morning, I walk up to a coffee stand on Abbot Kinney Boulevard, get in line, and order a black coffee for me and a caramel iced latte for Ellie.

"Can I get you anything else?" the helpful barista asks with a tilt of her freckled face.

I look down at Gigi, who's sitting perfectly by my feet. "A water for you, girl?"

Gigi pants. I take that as a yes. "One little paper cup of water for the pup, please?"

The barista flashes a warm smile. "Coming right up."

"I'm sooooo thirsty. Can I have one too?"

I groan, recognizing my friend Axel's voice despite the baby talk.

Busted.

With a *you caught me* sigh, I turn around and meet my buddy's dark, laughing gaze. "What are you doing here?"

Axel waggles his phone. "Catching that on video," he says, with a shit-eating grin. "This is the best."

I roll my eyes. "Seriously. Are you following me?"

He scoffs. "You're not *that* interesting." Then he tips his forehead across the street to another coffee shop, Edge & Plow. Because of course there's another coffee shop across the street. "Early bird and all. I got up at five AM to write. I had an idea. So I ran with it."

"Wait, let me guess. The hero breaks his dick during sex?"

"Wash your mouth out with soap," he says, chiding me.

"Come on. You're the king of writing *we fucked till we broke our arms* sex scenes."

"But nobody ever suffers from a broken dick in my books. What do you think I am, the world's meanest man?"

"Possibly," I say. Then I nod to his phone. "What are you going to do with that?"

His smile is evil. "No idea but this is gold. The big, bad wolf sweet-talking the little dog," he says, then tucks the phone in his jeans pocket and adjusts the strap on his messenger bag. "Also when did you get a dog? Were you going to keep it a secret? She's fucking adorable."

Like a proud papa, I scoop up the little blond creature, scratching Gigi's chin. She lifts it higher as I pet her. "She's Ellie's dog," I explain. "Isn't she cute?"

"Here are your drinks, Gabe," the barista says, then her smile widens, like she can't hold it in. "Go Mercenaries! I've got my lucky hacky sack too!"

With a smile, I rap my knuckles on the counter, then stuff an extra bill in the tip jar. "Keep kicking it! And thanks for the Mercenary love," I say as I set Gigi back down, then take all three drinks carefully. Once I turn the corner, I set the water cup for Gigi onto the sidewalk.

"Spill," Axel demands. "Who's Ellie?"

I'm not one to kiss and tell, so as Gigi laps up her drink, I answer him simply. "I grew up on the same street as Ellie. I ran into her again. There you go," I say but that barely covers who Ellie is.

She's vibrant, outgoing, and a sex kitten.

She's kind, thoughtful, and caring.

She's easy to spend time with. She's dirty and flirty and honest.

My heart thumps harder just thinking of my woman.

Axel clears his throat, then points to the dog,

who's finished her water. "You're walking her dog, man," he says as I bend to pick up the paper cup and crush it. I stuff it in my back pocket so I can toss it in the recycling at Ellie's house. "Ellie hardly seems like someone you 'just ran into,'" he says, sketching air quotes.

The dude is perceptive. But I'm not ready to let on to Axel that he's right. Not sure why though.

"The dog had to piss. Of course I took her with me," I say, trying to keep my answer simple.

Trying, but failing. I like her damn dog too.

That's fucking confusing.

"Dude, just admit you like her," Axel says as I walk toward Ellie's house.

"The dog is great," I say.

"I meant the woman. It sounds like someone has it bad," he mocks.

I grumble, "Goodbye, Axel." I'm just not ready to deal with the *someone has it bad* level of feels.

Or any level.

"You can't get rid of me that easily," Axel says. "Though actually, you will be getting rid of me soon. I'm going to Europe in a couple weeks to do some more research for my next thriller."

"I'd say I'll miss you but..."

"Fuck you. You'll miss me. I'll miss you, and I'm not afraid to say it."

"Fine. I'll miss you the tiniest little bit," I say.

We shoot the breeze as we walk the rest of the way to Ellie's house, and I'm grateful he doesn't press more. I don't know what I'd say, or if I could even articulate why I feel like she's my woman.

When she can't be.

She just fucking can't.

When I reach her home, I say goodbye to my friend. "I'll catch up with you later."

"Have fun with the...dog," Axel says with a wink.

Flipping him the bird, I head inside, cups in hand. Ellie's pacing the kitchen, her phone pressed to her ear. Brightly, she waves at me. Evidently, she's excited to see me and the dog.

My pulse skitters. I smile back at her as I unhook Gigi's leash from her harness, careful not to spill the drinks.

The dog scampers over to Ellie, whimpering happily as she dances on her back legs like it's been thirty years, and not thirty minutes since she's seen her person.

It's seriously the cutest thing. Especially when Ellie bends down to pet her. My woman's wearing yoga pants and a sports bra, and I like that outfit a lot.

So much it's scrambling my brain.

"Yes, Mom," she says into the phone, then pauses. "No, they haven't called again yet."

Another pause.

"I still don't know what to say if they want to interview me," she says with a sigh as I head into the kitchen and put the drinks on the counter, curious who she's talking about.

"Yes. I'll be there this weekend. *With Gabe,*" she adds with a hint of a smile in her voice.

Ah, I like the sound of that. There's a shriek on the other end of the line.

"Yes, Mom. *That Gabe.*"

I straighten my shoulders, pride surging through me. Yeah, I'm *that Gabe.* I'm that guy who's taking her to the party this weekend. No one else is taking her.

"Are we dating?" She arches a brow at me in question.

I growl, then give the only answer. I nod a clear and firm *yes.*

"We'll be on a date at your party," she says into the phone. "Love you too, Mom." Then she hangs up.

She doesn't say anything more to me about the dating comment. I'm not sure why, but I'm relieved. If she did, I might be tempted to tell her the truth—this sure as hell feels like real dating.

But real dating doesn't have an expiration date.

We do. We agreed to about a week. One week, one party, then we're done. Doesn't matter if I like her more and more each time we hang out.

I have training camp out of town starting in a few more days, and my final football season to focus on. I need to stay healthy and injury-free. That means no distractions.

She has her new gig writing and producing her show.

Case closed.

I wipe away thoughts of *more*, and *next week*, and *real dates*.

Ellie gestures to Gigi, who's trotting into the living room now. "You walked my dog." She says it like I've fought off lions.

Maybe that's what dog care is to her. The ultimate sign of devotion.

"And she really is a good girl," I say. I want to ask what she and her mom were talking about, but I don't know if we're at a "pry in your personal business" place.

But Ellie saves me from wondering, and shares, "My mom wanted to know if I'm going to do the interview." At my questioning look, she explains, "For the show *Fabio's List*." I'm still drawing a blank, but she goes on with the story of how she dated a guy who conned women and now LGO is doing a documentary about him.

Anger flares in my chest, hot and fast. "Did he hurt you?"

"Oh, no. Not like that. Not physically."

"Good. But I meant in any way. Did he hurt you

in any way?" I bite out. "Because I will fucking destroy him if he did."

Adamantly, she shakes her head. "No. He didn't hurt me emotionally too much either. And I got out early. I kind of spotted the signs that he was a con artist," she says, a touch of shame in her voice. "But I hate that he conned a bunch of other women." With a sigh, she lifts her caramel latte, and takes a sip. "So it just feels kind of raw. I think that's why I haven't said yes to the interview yet. I feel kind of foolish still."

Compelled to comfort her, I close the distance between us, move behind her, and press a kiss to her neck. I wrap my arms around her waist, holding her close. She sighs contentedly against me.

"Don't beat yourself up, sweetheart. Maybe dating some unsavory guys in the past helped you to see the signs with him. You figured out what to look for," I say, trying my damnedest to shore her up.

"Yeah, maybe. It's just too bad the other women didn't see that."

I nod resolutely. "It is. I hate men who take advantage of women. Who lie and cheat and steal. There's a special place in hell for them."

After she puts down the latte, she turns her face to me, a smile tipping her lips. My heart speeds up. Damn, her smile is magic, and she's casting a spell on me. "Thank you for the latte, Gabe. And for the dog walk. And just for saying that. I appreciate it."

I run a hand gently down her cheek. "I don't want anyone to hurt you ever." Then I brush my lips to hers. The kiss is soft and tender, and I like it far too much. So I linger in it, indulging in the taste of her caramel lips.

Axel's words echo in my head, taunting me. *Someone has it bad.*

But I bat them away. Of course I like her. Hell, I've liked her since that night under the mistletoe—the first night I *could* let myself like her.

That doesn't mean I can let anything happen beyond this week. A deal's a deal.

16

___

GOOD BEHAVIOR

A few hours later...

Gabe: That didn't take long.

Ellie: What? You returned home a few minutes ago, and you've already taken matters into your own hands?

Ellie: And I thought what I did to you this morning in the shower was enough...as well as on the kitchen floor after I finished the latte. Also under the covers in the middle of the night.

Ellie: But you do have a big appetite so...

Gabe: Damn, woman. You type too fast. And for the record, keep doing all of those things. I want them all. I *need* them all. But know this—if I jack off after I see you, it's because I am insatiable for you. And I am picturing the next thing we'll do. Like when I see you tonight.

Ellie: Acceptable answer.

Gabe: As I was trying to say, what didn't take long is that my mom already called. Guess she heard from your mom.

Ellie: Telephone works fast in our little hometown! Tongues are clearly wagging about our upcoming appearance this weekend.

Gabe: The book club ladies are buzzing about us. My mom called as I was heading to the gym. Wanted to talk all about you. I bet my dad will call any second too, since Mom tells him everything and vice versa.

Ellie: So what did your mom say? Did she give you a hard time? I hope not! *bites nails*

Gabe: No. Why would you say that?

Ellie: I guess maybe because I was the girl you babysat?

Gabe: And I was a perfect gentleman those nights. For the record, I never once thought of you naked until that eggnog party when you were in college, and you officially became the sexiest person I'd ever seen in my life.

Ellie: Wow. I'm flattered.

Gabe: It's the truth.

Ellie: For the record, you gave me my first orgasm when I was fifteen.

Gabe: WHAT???

Ellie: I had a crazy crush on you when I was a teenager.

Gabe: Whoa.

Ellie: Does that freak you out?

Gabe: Should it?

Ellie: I hope not. I truly hope not.

Gabe: Then it doesn't freak me out. Because you're all woman now, and I'm with the woman. Not the girl.

Ellie: *Breathes again* I was worried my teenage fantasies would scare you.

Gabe: We all have fantasies, sweetheart. It's what, when, and with whom we explore them that matters.

Ellie: I'm enjoying our explorations. I have fantasies about other scenarios. Student and teacher, strangers at a bar, you name it.

Gabe: Both sound fun, especially strangers at a bar. I'd say something like *Is this seat taken?*

Ellie: I'd say *now it is.* Bet we'd be great strangers. Then we'd get a cup of coffee in the morning, and I'd feel like we had a delicious secret.

Gabe: When I take you out in public, I get a thrill that I'm the only one who knows your private side.

Ellie: Me too.

Gabe: Can't wait to explore more tonight, my sweet, dirty girl.

Ellie: I'll be on my best behavior when I see you later.

Gabe: I won't.

17

YOU HAVE THE RIGHT

Gabe

Hands curled tightly around the wheel of my Tesla, I wait on the side of the road, on alert.

The faint glow from a streetlamp in the distance lights the curvy stretch of Mulholland Drive up here in the hills.

I have to tamp down this buzz of anticipation. Need to stay in the moment. Can't let the thrill of the fantasy get the better of me before she even arrives.

I check my phone. Her Google Map alert says she's almost here.

The second I hear the soft purr of an electric convertible winding around the bend, I start the engine.

It is on.

A few seconds later, she flies past me.

I jerk my car onto the road, gun the gas, and flash my headlights. Bright and fast in her rearview mirror.

She pulls into a turnout a hundred or so feet away.

I pull in behind her and cut the engine. My pulse is already spiking. I've wanted this for so damn long.

I've played in the goddamn Super Bowl, yet I'm somehow even more excited for this fantasy. I don't even know why. I just *want* this. So damn much.

I cut the engine and stride over to her, taking my sweet-ass time like a cop would do even though I want to touch her so damn badly.

When I reach the driver's side window, I tap on it.

She rolls it down, flashing an innocent but curious grin. "Was I speeding, officer?"

"You know you were," I tell her. "You got someplace to be?"

Her pretty pink lips form a taunting O. "I have to get to this hot guy's house. You understand, right?"

I grunt, then shake my head. "No," I say sternly. "You better not be speeding to get to some other man." I bend to lean on the window.

"But officer, he makes me sooo wet," she says, then subtly, ever so subtly, spreads her thighs.

A wild rumble fills my chest. She's going to test all my control.

"Get out," I command.

She bats her lashes. "But don't you want to see my license and registration? Or are you forgetting how to do your job?"

"Don't tell me how to do my job. For that, you need to spread your legs," I order.

"Ooh, you're a bad cop," she says, nibbling on the corner of her lips.

"And you're a bratty girl," I say, then grab the handle and yank open the door. "Out. Now."

With a defiant stare, she rises, stands in front of me, and crosses her arms, pushing up those glorious tits.

Dear god.

She's wearing the world's shortest skirt, along with the universe's sexiest heels.

"My guy won't like that you called me bratty," she taunts.

"You broke the speed limit, miss." I step closer, drag my nose along her neck, inhaling her cherry blossom scent. It drives me wild. "Go around to the other side of the vehicle," I tell her.

"What if I don't want to? Will you put these on me?" She darts out with nimble fingers and grabs a pair of cuffs from my back pocket.

New ones. I bought them today. *For her.* And I

fucking tremble as I picture putting them on her and then torturing her deliciously with my hands.

She dangles the cuffs in front of me, the temptress.

I snatch them from her. "Move. Now."

"If you say so," she says, then struts around the back of the car, shaking that perfect ass.

Desire claws at me. But we're not even close to ending the scene yet. I fight off the cloud of lust, stalk around the back of the car, and come right up to her, my chest against hers, all of Los Angeles below us, the city lights twinkling in the distance.

But here on the side of the road, it's quiet enough. Even though anyone could come by. What a rush. "Turn around, miss. Spread your legs."

She whirls, reaches for the hem of her skirt, lifts it.

My skin sizzles. She's wearing white lace panties that barely cover her luscious cheeks.

I want to bite that sweet ass.

But she's so damn defiant. "I said...spread them," I grit out.

She flashes her vixen gaze my way. "Make me, officer."

Need swamps me. I step closer, between her legs, then kick her right foot. Then her left.

She gasps but doesn't stumble as she widens her stance. My chest heaves with want. And my mind floods with understanding. I know why I want *this* fantasy.

I crave trust. Always have. It's not only the foundation of my job—it's the cornerstone of any relationship. That's what I've seen from the people around me. The way they trust and depend on each other.

But now, I'm seeing trust in another light. A smoky, sexy light.

An after-dark one, with a woman who trusts me to test her, to push her, to take care of her.

Ellie trusts me so beautifully, which turns me on more than her beautiful body. Her trust in me thrills me to my bones.

And I intend to treat it like the gift it is. "You're under arrest," I command.

"Good," she taunts.

I grab her wrists and yank them together. Hold them tightly in my grip. With my other hand, I snap on the cuffs. God, she looks stunning, at my mercy like this. Offering me her body. Her voice. And her beautiful, dirty mind. To do with what I will.

My skin heats with excitement.

"So this guy you were dying to see," I say sternly as I lock the cuffs.

"Yes, officer?"

"You needed to drive that fast to see him?"

"He's sexy and growly and ridiculously possessive," she says in a sensual purr.

I jerk on the cuffs. "Does he give it to you good?"

She trembles. "He fucks me till I scream," she whispers.

I growl, then slide my hands over the soft, tempting flesh of her ass, squeezing both cheeks. "Is that any way to talk to an officer of the law?"

"Maybe you should take me in for the night. Lock me up."

That's it. I'm about to snap with lust. I press my body to hers, my hard-on grinding against her ass. "You have the right to remain aroused," I whisper hotly into her ear.

She arches against me.

"Anything you say can and will be used against you by me as I get you off," I say.

"Play with my pussy, officer," she says, going with our roles so perfectly. "Use your hand and make me come."

I slide a palm between her thighs, gliding my fingers across the soaked panel of her panties.

She rocks against me, then pants, "Tease my clit, officer."

She rocks and thrusts, and I glide my finger under the slippery lace and across her hot center. When I reach her clit, she drops her head back and groans.

Too loud.

Roughly, like she wants it, I clamp a hand over her mouth. She gasps. Arches. Seeks more of my hand. "This'll teach you to obey the law," I say as I stroke her sweet clit.

She writhes against my palm.

I go faster, following her cues, reading her pleasure.

This wicked thrill is *everything*.

She rocks shamelessly as I play with her wet pussy until she's moaning and riding my hand.

I'm strung tight as I stroke her.

With a bitten-off groan, she comes, her whole body shaking beautifully.

I let go of her wrists, unlock her, and spin her around. She's never looked more beautiful than she does now, on the side of the road, trusting me to make her feel incredible. "I think I'll need to keep you overnight, miss," I rasp out.

With a woozy, satisfied smile, she says, "You better." Then she murmurs, "Thank you."

She's thanking me? I should be building her a shrine, getting down on my knees in gratitude to her for letting me fuck her the way I've always wanted to.

My heart hammers. "No. Thank you, sweetheart."

We drive in separate cars to her home, and once we're inside, I kiss her deeply, passionately. Then I take her to bed and slide inside her. She wraps her arms around me and pulls me close.

"I like this overnight," she says.

But I want to keep her more than overnight. I want to tell her what she's doing to me. And that's getting to be a big fucking problem.

FRIDAY

A Day for Confessions

18

CAN'T GET MY MIND OFF YOU

The Next Morning

Gabe: Wow. Last night was incredible.

Ellie: I know! I feel a little high still from the side of the road.

Gabe: I have a confession.

Ellie: Tell me.

Gabe: I've wanted to do that for so long.

Ellie: Yeah?

Gabe: Yes. It's been an ultimate fantasy. But then, so are you.

Ellie: I'm blushing.

Gabe: And here's the thing—I'm so fucking glad it was you.

Ellie: I'm so glad it was me too.

Gabe: The whole night was amazing. Back at your house.
You're a dream, Ellie. The morning was pretty great too.

Ellie: Well, you do make good dairy-free pancakes. You're a man of many talents. :)

Gabe: Anything for you. I can't wait to see you tonight.

Ellie: Same here. I want to see you.

Gabe: Ellie?

Ellie: Yeah?

Gabe: I can't stop thinking about you.

19

———

MONSTER FEELINGS

Ellie

I've been texting Gabe as I walk to Maddox's home, but we finish chatting right when I reach my friend's place. I'm still giddy from the conversation. Probably glowing too.

When Maddox opens the door to his home a few seconds later, my friend sizes me up quickly. "Let me guess. You either just saw the bad boy, talked to him, or you were texting with him."

Yup. Giddy and glowing.

"Stop being so good at reading me," I say, then tuck my phone into my bag, and sweep into his house.

"I'm good at reading *all* people," he says, then

shuts the door behind us. "I have to be. It's why I'm good at my job."

From someone else, that comment might come across as conceited. But Maddox says it matter-of-factly. It's just the truth of who he is and how he operates.

"It *is* your special skill. And Gabe and I were just texting as I walked here."

"Called it."

"I know," I say, then I squeeze his arm. "Thanks for inviting me over." I pat my messenger bag and the canvas bag alongside it. "I've got my laptop and my bathing suit."

"What else does anyone ever need?" He smiles softly. "Thanks for coming."

He lives nearby so we decided to work together today. He'll be writing contracts, and I'll be tweaking the script for episode one of *The Dating Games*. After we head through his sleek, minimalist home, we settle in poolside, where he serves me iced tea at a table under an umbrella. I take a drink and point at the glass approvingly. "You are an iced tea wizard," I say.

"Thanks. But enough about me. What's the deal with the bad boy? Gabe, you said?"

My stomach swoops as I think of the man who's captured my nights and mornings. "Here's the thing. Gabe kind of seems like a bad boy, but he's really a great guy. Gabe Clements," I add, sharing his full name since there's no reason to be coy. Gabe and I have been going out in public, after all. "He takes my dog out for walks in the morning while I'm sleeping. He brings me the lattes I like. He listens when I talk. He asks questions about my friends and my job, and he pays attention, and he's thoughtful," I say, my heart fluttering ridiculously.

"So, that's...good?" Maddox asks carefully. Then, he adds more decisively, "Because it sounds great to me."

Huh.

That does all sound great. Surprisingly so. I suppose I didn't expect this one-week deal to be so... *good* outside of the bedroom. I figured we'd indulge in sex, but I didn't anticipate liking Gabe's company so much. "Yeah, it is great," I say, a little wary, because...hello. We made a deal. One that ends tomorrow night at Aunt Tilly's party. "But it's early days. That's just how it goes. Honeymoon phase and all." I wave a hand airily, trying to dismiss these pesky feelings.

Maddox chuckles. But says nothing.

I huff. "All right, friend. What are you *not* saying?"

Another laugh, then he turns serious. "I'm saying that I think first impressions matter. I think the spark, the connection, the intensity—that's meaningful. I think, too, that everything you said about him—walking your dog, listening, caring—that's not honeymoon-level stuff. That's *real*."

Oh, shit.

He's right.

I sang Gabe's praises like those things he did were nothing. They're *not* nothing. They're wonderful. But there's no room to linger on how wonderful since Gabe and I have an end date.

"Maybe," I say, then run my finger along the rim of the iced tea glass, trying to sort through the ping-pong game my feelings are playing.

"Ellie," Maddox chides, seeing right through me. "This guy sounds like more than a maybe."

Ugh. Why does he have to be so right? I toss my hands up in the air, giving in. "Fine, you're right. I like him. There. Are you happy?"

He laughs again. "Don't ever change."

"I won't," I say, playfully defiant. Then I relent. I'm not a secret keeper. Not from my friends. "We fit. We just fit so well," I admit, relieved to stop fighting my feelings. Well, for a second at least. "Do you know what I mean?"

A look of longing flashes in Maddox's warm brown eyes. "I do," he says a little wistfully.

But there's a hint of pain in his voice too that worries me. I cover his hand with mine. "Did I touch a nerve?"

"No." He sighs and slumps back in his chair. "It's fine."

Wait. Hold on. He's notoriously private about his romantic life. For him to even say *it's fine* is revealing. "Maddox...have you met a guy you like?"

His resigned smile is answer enough. Judging from his expression, whatever happened with this guy isn't still happening.

"I did," he says, a big admission for him. "But it can't work out." He's resolute, but I can hear, too, that he's trying to be strong.

"Why can't it work out?" I ask desperately because I feel it desperately. I want all the good things for my friends. I want Maddox to have mad, passionate, soul-deep love.

He takes a beat, dragging a hand through his hair, then taking his time as he answers with, "It's complicated. And risky. And probably a bad idea."

I frown then squeeze his hand harder. "This guy sounds great actually."

Maddox cracks up, a deep laugh that seems to move through his body. "I haven't told you a thing about him."

"And yet I still know," I say. Maddox might be careful with his words, but he's not the only intuitive one. "I can read people too."

He smirks. "And what's the story in the book of me that you're reading, Ellie?"

I point at his chest. "I think he sounds great because it sounds like you have big, monster feelings," I say, my eyebrows arching in query. "Feelings you have to fight off."

He sighs. Long, maybe a little frustrated. "It doesn't matter," he says, his tone concise, ending the conversation about his mystery man. "Enough about me. Tell me more about your guy and *your* monster feelings."

"No way do I have monster feelings," I say with a scoff. But my heart is drumming a little harder, a little faster.

Stupid heart. Stupid feelings.

Maddox snorts.

"I admitted I like him," I say, with an *I've given in already* smile. "Do you want me to serve my heart up on a platter?"

"That's the idea."

I roll my eyes.

Maddox doesn't back down. Just keeps his gaze locked on me. "You like him. He's good people. So what's the problem? Seriously? Everything sounds great."

My heart pangs, the start of an ache. But there's no space for heartache when we're ending too damn soon.

I take a fueling breath to reset since the answer is simple. The problem is neither Gabe nor I want more. We're both devoted to other things. "I need to focus on my show, and he needs to focus on football," I say, chin up, armor on. "It's an important year for him and it's a critical time for me. And we both just got out of bad relationships so…"

"Timing. Circumstances," Maddox says sagely, getting it.

"Yeah. They're not lining up. So it's best to just focus on work," I say, bright and cheery.

Like I have to be.

I do love my job. I *am* excited about it.

And hell, I moved across the country for this. I should concentrate on my monster feelings for *The Dating Games.*

For the next few hours, I dig into the script as he works on deals. We order lunch, and as we eat our quinoa bowls, I show him a scene. He laughs as he reads it. "That is a most excellent dating challenge. Try something that scares you," he says with a smile. "I can't wait to see it on air."

As the sun travels across the summer sky, we take a break, changing into our swimsuits and jumping into the pool.

I chat about Los Angeles and my new home and Gigi, doing my best to help keep his mind off his romantic woes. Mine too. But now and then, he gets a faraway look in his eyes. Maybe soon he'll tell me more about his guy and what went down.

When we're done swimming, I change back into street clothes, twist my hair into a tie, then pack up my computer. As Maddox walks me out, I check my email on my phone. "Oh," I say, stopping in the front hallway, surprised to see a message from Sidney Stinson. The producer of *Fabio's List* wrote to me again.

I read it out loud to Maddox. "I'd really love to chat with you for our doc, Ellie. I know it's a sensitive topic and you're understandably cautious, but I promise to treat the interview with respect and gravitas. If you're willing, I'd love to hear back by Monday to set things in motion." I finish the note with nerves flickering through me. When I'm done, I meet Maddox's steady gaze. "What do you think? Should I do it?"

Maddox has such a level head, and he's always given solid business advice. "If it matters to you," he says diplomatically.

Does this show matter to me? Does the topic speak to me? "I didn't want to at first, but I'm actually sort of considering it now. Gabe gave me some good advice on it this morning," I say.

Maddox smiles and then rubs my shoulder. "This guy sounds good for you?" His voice pitches up at the end, making it a question. *Could it ever work out with Gabe?*

But I know the answer—I can't start to rely on Gabe too much.

I have friends like Maddox to turn to. He'll be in my life after this week and Gabe will return to the friends-of-the-family zone. He'll be someone I see once or twice a year over eggnog and veggie barbecues.

As I walk home, I tap out a reply to the producer. *I'll think about it over the next few days.*

Then I set myself a reminder to follow-up. So I don't become one of those people who leaves other producers hanging. That's not who I want to be, and I don't want to treat Sidney that way.

There. That's done. I'll put it out of my mind for the rest of the night.

Tonight is for my last private date with Gabe.

That's a sobering thought, that we're ending our fling after the party tomorrow.

But I don't want to get all up in my feels on our last evening together when it's just us. Besides, all good things end, I suppose. My time in New York came to an end. My show *Unfinished Business* lasted a few seasons. My friendships are shifting.

It's fine.

It's all just fine.

Once I'm at my house, I let Gigi out for a quick bathroom break, shower, and pull on a red tank top that shows off my stomach. Then a cute black skirt. I show Gigi the outfit, and I'm sure she approves.

After I swipe on some makeup, I flash back on Gabe's text from earlier.

When I take you out in public, I get a thrill that I'm the only one who knows the private side of you.

That thrills me too, so I pack a little something extra for tonight in a canvas bag.

Then I take my favorite person for a walk. Gigi struts around Venice Beach in her pink rhinestone harness, looking like the badass queen of California. We walk along the main drag, checking out storefronts, soaking in the vibe—the street is teeming with artsy types with colorful tattoos and copious bangles, surfer dudes with long hair and smoothies, and guys and gals in tailored business attire too.

"This is our new home, girl. I'll find all my story inspiration here," I say as we near The Happiest Hours. That was the bar where I saw Gabe a few nights ago— that set these nights of play into motion. I didn't notice the bar had a back patio the first time I walked past it. But there are ping-pong tables set up and a handful of women in shorts and bikinis are playing the game, trash talking each other. I love a game of ping-pong, so I'll have to return sometime soon. Does Gabe play ping-pong? He's an athlete, so I bet he'd have a blast playing.

It'd be fun to return with him.

Cool it, Ellie.

That's not what our fling is about.

I'll return with...Maddox. Yes, a friends' night out will be good. I head down the block, nearing Rachel's jewelry shop. Maybe she'll play.

The sign on the window says, "Well-behaved four-legged friends are welcome."

"That's you," I say to Gigi, then scoop her up and head inside.

"Hi, new friend," I call out. "Do you play ping-pong?"

Rachel looks up from her tablet on the counter, then brightens. There must be a lull in traffic since her boutique is mostly empty. "Hey, you! Good to see you again, Ellie. And yes, I do," she says, then eyes me up and down. "Someone's going on a date tonight."

"Is it that obvious?"

"You have a pre-date glow about you," she says.

"Maybe I'll have a post-date one too," I say in a conspiratorial whisper.

"Get it, girl," she says.

"I plan to."

"Good for you. Moving to a new town and dating right away." She flicks her brown hair off her shoulders, then shudders. "It's scary out there, but you're diving in. I admire that. Lord knows, I don't have the guts to do it."

A smidge of guilt wiggles around inside me. I'm

not *quite* diving into it. I don't want people to think I'm good at this dating thing when I'm sort of a sham.

"Well, not exactly," I say, feeling a little sheepish.

Maybe I should tell her the truth. I don't want anyone to think I'm some kind of example of go-getter womanhood when I'm just playing a game. One with rules and a clock.

But the bell tinkles above the store and a pack of customers strides in. This is not the time nor place to issue a correction.

Instead, as Rachel heads over to help them, I peruse the necklaces by the counter, then pick a silver chain with a small typewriter charm.

I show it to my pup. "Do you approve?"

She rubs her head against me.

"Excellent," I say, then when Rachel swings by again, I pay for the necklace and thank her.

"Let me know how the date goes," she says. "I'm surviving on secondhand date fumes."

I laugh. "I will. Want to do dinner on Sunday? We can catch up on all the things," I say.

"Is there ping-pong involved too?"

"That can be arranged."

"I'm there," she says, and we agree to meet at Max's Restaurant on Sunday, then hit The Happiest Hours. I'll tell her then that I'm not a bold dating icon. I'm just a woman who's having a little fun. *Had.*

By then I'll be a woman who has *had* a little fun, past tense.

I leave and head home, but I don't feel entirely satisfied.

I feel *off*.

I wasn't as honest as I want to be with friends.

Inside my house, as I give Gigi a fresh bowl of water in her *I Wish I Could Text My Dog* bowl, I make a new plan—I'll text Rachel later and let her know that my date tonight is just a fun thing, nothing to be admired.

That feels less squicky. More honest.

With a sense of relief, I check the time. I need to take off to meet Gabe, so I round the kitchen counter to shut my laptop. The scene where I left off earlier catches my eye, and I read it again.

By the power vested in me as your bestie, I hereby order you to take a new dating challenge, the hero says.

Give the order, the heroine replies.

Do something that scares you.

Perhaps it's time I take my heroine's challenge tonight—try something that scares me.

I don't mean in bed, though. I mean *before*.

20

PRACTICE MAKES PERFECT

Ellie

The thing about a honeymoon is it's temporary. Then you go back to real life and make the relationship work when you don't have room service.

No matter what Maddox says about how great Gabe is for me, we only have a honeymoon. There's no relationship to make work.

But even though this is a temporary fling, I can tell Gabe *something* tonight. Something real. I'm still working out what to say exactly though as I hunt for a parking spot at the park.

That's the challenge I set for myself tonight. Be more than sexy. Be *vulnerable.*

I find a parking spot, cut the engine, and grab the two slices of pie I picked up for our evening picnic.

I get out of the red convertible, then shield my eyes against the fading sun. I peer past a group of guys in their thirty-somethings playing volleyball, then some college dudes tossing a frisbee.

In the distance are picnic tables, and a six-foot-three, strapping, tattooed man unpacking food at one of them.

My heart scampers in my chest. My skin warms. Is this infatuation? Or more? I just like him so much I barely know what to do with these feelings.

Is that what I want to say?

Hey, Gabe, I dig you.

Hey, handsome, I'm totally into you.

Hey there, this has been the best week ever and I'm not just saying that because of your dick.

Yeah, maybe not those.

I'll need to workshop this confession like it's a scene in my TV show. But as I cross the park, I hit pause in my *scare myself into opening up* challenge when my gaze catches on a wicker basket on the table. Then the red checked tablecloth underneath it. And, at last, I settle on the man.

Sure, I knew we were having a picnic, but I didn't expect him to have an actual picnic basket. It's such an incongruous image—the big, burly man reaching into the old-fashioned basket.

And it gives me butterflies.

How will he react when I tell him I like him? I think he might like me too, but he was so clear about the week limit. But that's why I'm going to take my own challenge.

Toting a pink pie box and a belly full of nerves, I cross the final stretch of spongy grass, then reach him. After I set down the pie box, I point, flabbergasted, at the spread. "You have a basket."

"Don't tell a soul," he says gruffly as he takes out a container of olives, putting them next to some Marcona almonds. They're keeping company with hummus, carrots, and blueberries. My mouth waters.

"Your secret is safe with me," I say, then I lift my chin in a very obvious request for a kiss.

I need a kiss for courage.

He hauls me in for a hot, searing one while his hand grips the small of my back. He devours my mouth. This is not a picnic kiss. It's nightclub devastation. We're not a red-and-white-checked-tablecloth kind of couple. We are satin sheets and blindfolds.

When we separate, I'm dizzy. Then, my pulse soars when he slides a hand down my back again, stopping at my ass, spreading his hand across it. He squeezes, harder than he has before.

Wild thoughts race through my mind.

New ideas.

New fantasies.

Ones that kick things up another notch.

When I take you out in public, I get a thrill that I'm the only one who knows the private side of you.

Yes, I know what I want in bed tonight. Something that makes me even more vulnerable.

"I like the basket," I say in a low and sensual voice, but I'm not just talking about the accouterment. I'm talking about *him.* I cover his hand on my ass with mine, pressing his palm more firmly against my flesh.

His eyes glimmer. "I can tell," he says, and the double meaning isn't lost on him. Then he grabs me roughly.

I gasp.

When he lets go, he kisses me once more. This one is sweet. Like icing. Maybe now is the time to say: *this is more than fun and games for me.*

He tips his forehead to the table. "I bought the basket for you today. As part of our practice," he says.

He bought a picnic basket.

For me.

He shopped for vegan food.

For me.

I can't ignore the happy bubbles floating up through my bloodstream any longer.

I made a promise to be real tonight, and it terrifies me. But that's the point. "Gabe," I say tentatively as someone in the volleyball game shouts, *Nice one.*

"What is it, sweetheart?" he asks.

I'm shaking with nerves, but I've gone on stage and performed for thousands. I can confess how I feel to one man.

I gulp, then think, *Screw the nerves.* "I'm having such a great time with you, and I just wanted to let you know—"

"Duck!" someone shouts.

I flinch at the warning, spin around for the shouter when I see a red frisbee's flying right at Gabe's head, like a missile.

"Gabe!" I cry out, but he's already blocking, shoving his body in front of me, and sticking out his right arm.

Then *boom.*

He catches the frisbee before it whacks his head.

My pulse is racing when a guy—maybe twenty—stops short, panting. "I'm so sorry," he says.

Gabe tilts his head, studies the guy with dark, angry eyes. Ohhhh. Is he going to rip this guy to pieces like he did the redhead at the bar?

"You almost hit my woman," he warns in a low voice.

My woman.

Gawd. Those words heat me up. Gabe doesn't even care that the frisbee was heading for him. He's bothered that I might have been collateral damage.

The guy turns to me, his eyes guilty. "I'm really sorry. I was just playing a game."

He sounds so earnest, so devastated.

"I'm fine. We're fine," I say.

Then Gabe breathes out like he's letting go of the irritation. "Yeah, just be more careful," Gabe says, and he's no longer the man about to rip off heads. He knows how to handle situations. He knows when to issue a warning and when to go caveman.

As the guy trots off with the frisbee, Gabe turns to me, concern etched in his irises. "You okay, sweetheart?"

My heart is sprinting. "I'm great," I say.

He runs a hand gently down my hair. "You sure?"

"I am," I say, resolute.

"Good," he says, then kisses my forehead before sitting down. I join him. "You were saying something?" he prompts.

I'm so frothy and turned on I don't remember what had been on the tip of my tongue. I need a moment to reset. "Just...this is nice. This is all really nice," I say, gesturing to the picnic.

"Good. You deserve nice things," he says.

Nice things like him?

Deliberately, I recall the purpose of our deal. We're here to practice for the party. Maybe it's best if I zoom in on that while I clear my head of that uptick in desire from seconds ago. I pluck a blueberry from the carton and pop it in my mouth. "And we're supposed to be a nice girl and boy tomorrow night," I say.

"I don't think the cop scene last night was very good practice."

I laugh. "Not one bit...So, let's pretend Aunt Tilly just asked how we met again."

But Gabe doesn't take the bait. He eats a few olives with a thoughtful frown. "Actually, I don't want to practice for the party right now."

I sit up straighter. "Oh. Why?" My radar beeps in a gentle warning.

"About last night..."

Does he regret the role play? I ask warily, "What about it?"

"It was incredible—like I told you then. Like I told you again this morning." He's emphatic and reaches for my hand, threading his fingers through mine. "And I keep thinking about why. Why I liked it so much. Besides the obvious."

"That it was hot?" I ask.

"Yes. Besides that," he says, his tone still serious. "And I started thinking about that first night we went out." He draws what sounds like a steadying breath. "I was planning to leave you when we got to your house."

I flinch. Maybe it's a good thing I haven't told him my feelings. "You were?"

"I was trying to exit gracefully," he admits, and I'm not sure I like where this is going. "I was sure if you knew I liked it rough, you'd throw a shoe at me."

My worry slinks away, replaced only by concern. I wish he hadn't felt that way, even for a brief while. "Why would you think that?"

He swallows and glances away like maybe he's embarrassed. "My ex did," he mutters. "And I thought if you knew what I wanted to do to you, that you might chuck your helmet and scooter at me."

"Oh Gabe," I say gently, feeling terrible that he thought that even for a few hours. "No, of course not. But what happened with her?"

He's quiet for several long seconds. Then he answers heavily. "I asked to spank her, and she just freaked out. That's why we split. I mean, it's for the best. At first, I thought we were a good fit. It's not like the bedroom issue was some deal breaker for me when I started seeing her. But over time, she started questioning me and accusing me of being interested in other women."

I snort. I literally snort. "You're pretty single-minded, as far as I can tell."

He kisses my cheek like my compliment means everything to him. "Damn right, I am." He sighs and goes back to his story. "But it just told me we didn't have a lot of trust. I guess I thought we could build it in the bedroom. But when I asked, she lost her shit and went off on me loud enough to let my neighbors know she thought I was a pervert. I felt stupid, and honestly, kind of awful," he says, wincing. He's still feeling the sting of that indignity she'd dealt him?

I run my hand through his hair, comforting him. "I hate that you felt that way," I say.

"Thanks. I even got her handcuffs as a gift, thinking it could help." He gives a humorless laugh.

I linger on what he just told me about handcuffs, then on his text messages earlier about how it was an ultimate fantasy for him. I get it now. Last night *was* a big deal for him.

"And just so you know, I bought the ones from last night just for you," he says, and the self-mocking tone has vanished. There's a fierceness in its place. "I'd never use secondhand cuffs on you."

I smile softly, then he continues.

"Anyway, when we split up, Brittany's sister came to get her things, and she shoved the cuffs at me like they were diseased. Like I was a freak."

My heart squeezes. "Sex is so much more than bodies tangled together. It's about our hearts, and our minds too."

His sigh sounds relieved. "Yeah. It is, Ellie."

"It's about desire and freedom and need," I say, unable to let it go.

"Yes." He nods in strenuous agreement. "You're saying exactly what I'm feeling. But see, when I met you again, I thought if you knew how I liked to fuck, you'd rip me to shreds."

I rest my head on his shoulder. "I'm sorry she made you feel that way. I like everything about the way you touch me. Actually, I *love* the way you touch me."

He wraps an arm around my shoulders. "I love touching you. I'm glad you told me how you like it. You're a fucking dream, Ellie," he says, that rough and smoky tone returning to his voice.

I pull away so I can meet his eyes. "I'm glad I told you too. And thank you for being honest with me."

And finally, *I know*.

I know what the *be vulnerable* challenge means to me.

Being real doesn't mean I have to say *I like you*.

It's obvious we like each other. There's something deeper at play with Gabe. Something that matters more.

"Gabe, these last three nights have been incredible," I begin.

"They have," he says, tightening his grip on my hand.

"And I've had some trust issues with guys. A lot of trust issues, to be honest. I've picked poorly before, like I told you. But it's different with you."

A small smile forms on his lips. "Yeah?"

I nod. "I trust you so much," I say, and finally, this feels right.

This admission is scary.

But it's true, and it's something I want him to know. "I feel safe with you, Gabe. At first, I didn't know the reason—I just felt it. *Safety*."

"Good. I want you to."

"But now I know why," I say, giddy with understanding.

"Tell me."

"Because of how you treat me out of bed. You treat me like a queen," I say, holding his gaze. "And that's why I feel safe with you. I've always been fascinated with my own limits," I say, and I'm not scared anymore. It's a thrill to tell him my truth. It's freeing to share my desires with a man who wants me to feel safe all the time, in and out of bed. "And there's one more thing I've been wanting to try," I say.

"Anything. Tell me anything," he says, desperate.

I take a beat, run a hand down his arm. "I'll tell you...in confession."

21

———

FORGIVE ME, FATHER

Gabe

Her heels click against the white tiled floor, then the sound muffles when she comes into my bedroom, the plush carpet absorbing the noise. She must have brought those shoes with her. She wore sandals at the park. She packed for this scene, and that excites me.

Seated in a high-back chair on one side of the open closet door, I'm wearing a black button-down and slacks. My priest costume.

There's a chair on the other side of the door.

"Good evening, Father," she says, in a soft voice.

"Good evening," I say as she sits.

"Bless me, Father, for I have sinned," she begins,

her tone contrite. "It's been...oh gosh. Oh no." She sounds so terribly worried. "Actually, I don't know how long it's been since my last confession." She lets out a shuddery breath. "I can't focus though. I can't think."

This wasn't scripted. But fuck it. She's always been the director of our scenes, throwing me for loops. She makes the choices. I just roll with them. "Why can't you think, my child?"

"Because...Father," she says, her tone a little trembly. "I don't think I've seen you here before."

It comes out borderline sensual.

"I'm new," I improvise.

"Ohh. That's good to know," she says, breathy, almost a purr.

This woman is going to push all my buttons tonight. When Ellie role-plays, she fucking plays. She is all in. And I have to hold my own. Adjust to her character. Clearing my throat, I adopt a stern voice. Tonight, I'll be the merciless priest.

"Why don't you start by confessing your biggest sins," I command.

There's a rustle of clothes. The sound of movement. She's fidgeting with something, maybe that new necklace she's wearing tonight. "Gosh, there are so many, Father. I don't know where to begin. I've had such a busy week."

Me fucking too.

I tug on my collar, like that'll turn down the temperature that's rising in me. "Start with your sins from the last week, my child."

"Are you sure? I was pretty bad. Do you want them all?" There's a teasing lilt to her words.

"Yes, I want them all," I say crisply, matching her vixen with my domination. "Start now."

I can't see her face, but I can see her legs. She crosses those toned calves, one heel resting on the other.

My breath races along with my thoughts. Those legs spread-eagled on my bed. Those heels on my shoulders. Her standing in front of the bathroom mirror.

It's like she can read my mind, the way she rubs the red toe of her shoe against the inside of her calf. "I had impure thoughts about a man," she begins, like she regrets her dirty mind.

"Just thoughts? Tell the truth, my child," I order.

I can hear her swallow nervously. "Fine. They were more than thoughts."

I sit up straighter. "Tell me what you did. Don't leave out a single, salacious detail," I tell her. "This is your penance. You must confess every filthy, lascivious tidbit."

She lets out a nervous breath. "He spanked me, Father. And I liked it. I liked it so much when he hit me, and he marked me, and he made me hiss," she coos in a rush.

And the temperature hits Death Valley levels or higher. The admission that she likes it—even though I know, I fucking know, I was there—cranks my engine.

I adjust myself in my seat, then hiss out in a mean voice, "You'll need penance for that, but I can't give it to you until you finish describing all of your grievous sexual sins to me."

She gasps. "As you wish, Father."

Ellie goes on to recount our nights in excruciatingly sensual detail, torturing me with her story of the filthy, beautiful sex we had. As she talks, my head goes hazy with longing. My chest tightens, glowing with this slow-burning fire.

I ball my hands into fists.

She's seducing me all over again with the story of us, and I want to lunge at her and punish her with pleasure.

This time with her has been such a rush, such a wicked thrill. These last few nights have been a revelation. But I try to stay in the moment, not get lost in the haze of my own aching desire for her. When she's done, I dig my nails into my palms as I ask, "And what else, my child? What else do you want to confess?"

She sighs nervously, making little gaspy noises like she's struggling as she leans into her role as the naughty penitent. I bet she's nibbling on that gorgeous lower lip. "Father, that's only the start. There's something else I can't stop thinking about. Those impure thoughts I mentioned? I need to tell them to you. Now."

There she goes again, wrestling all the control. "Tell me your impure thoughts so I can absolve you."

"Well," she says, stretching out her legs now, giving me a full view of those gorgeous limbs, "it's more like a fantasy."

My chest is a furnace. "Go on."

"They're about you, Father," she whispers. "I want you to..." She stops. Then she goes quiet. I don't say a word. I just wait for her.

Then she's barely audible.

I'm not even sure I heard right. That two-word command.

"Excuse me?"

She clears her throat. "Leave marks," she says, no more whispering now. "Hit me with a paddle and mark me."

Holy. Fuck.

I stand, breaking character, coming to face her. I get down on my knees, looking at her wide eyes. "You do, sweetheart?"

Her lower lip quivers but with anticipation. Her irises seem to gleam with...wicked excitement.

"Remember when you texted me—*When I take you out in public, I get a thrill that I'm the only one who knows the private side of you.*"

I nod quickly. "Yes," I say eagerly, dying to know what's next.

She swallows, then lifts her chin. "I want you to bruise me. I want to look in the mirror as I get ready for the party tomorrow and see marks. *Your marks.* I've never done that."

God, I want this so fucking badly. But there's one problem. "I don't have anything to use. I don't know if I can leave marks like that with my hand." I think quickly. What do I have? "But I can look in the kitchen. Maybe a spatula. A wooden spoon."

Her lips curve into a dirty smirk. "I brought a paddle."

My eyes squeeze shut for a second. I'm light-headed with lust. But that's barely the beginning. I'm overwhelmed with emotions too. New ones, surprising ones.

But ones I'll have to deal with later. First, I need to deal with her.

I open my eyes and take back control. "Say a prayer, my child. You're going to take your penance bent over the counter. Ass raised. For me."

Ellie's brown eyes twinkle, then she darts out a hand, runs it across my chin. "You are such a hot priest."

22

A PING-PONG KIND OF THING

Ellie

I didn't come to Los Angeles to explore all my wild sex fantasies.

I came to this town to work.

But on the cusp of the biggest week in my career, I'm gripping the edge of the kitchen counter, and he's railing me.

With a vicious grip on my hips, he fucks me deeper, harder, alternating spanks with tugs on my hair.

A sharp slap tears through me, the pain blooming into pleasure. I moan, a savage sound ripped from my soul.

Then, he whispers darkly in my ear, "You ready, baby?"

Like I've never been before. "So ready."

He eases back, reaches for the ping-pong paddle on the counter, and lifts it. But I can't see him, so I don't know when it's coming.

He pushes deep into me, then out, then *whack.*

The paddle stings.

The pain bursts.

And I jump. "Oh, god," I gasp.

"Okay?"

But then I'm moaning because I'm warm all over.

"Yes," I say.

He sinks into me again, one hand snaking around my waist, down to my clit.

As he rubs, I rock back against his cock, murmuring into the exquisite bliss of his fingers.

Then...*smack.*

A hard sting. The sharp ache spreads through my body chased by a burst of desire.

Then a luxurious wave of sensations saying *more, more.*

"Again," I beg in a whisper.

He teases my clit with his fingers, pinching me, then hitting me.

Sharp. Hard. Deliciously.

"Oh god," I yelp.

"Do you need me to stop?" he asks.

"I need you to do it again. Both sides. Mark me the same," I urge, my voice a barren pant.

He grunts like an animal. "Fuck, Ellie."

Then he pounds into me, smacking my other cheek with the paddle. Pain shatters under his touch, but I rock back into his thrusts, seeking that moment when it crests and breaks into this...bliss.

He paddles one cheek, then the other.

Soon, I'm lost in a trance. The sensations of pleasure and pain flip every few seconds, one chasing the other, one turning into the other.

I ask for more, and he gives me what I want until the pain overwhelms me. It's too much and I hit my limit.

"Scooter," I whisper desperately.

Immediately, he sets the paddle on the counter and slows his pace. "What do you need, baby? I'll give you anything," he rasps out.

I need speed. Intensity. I need to be fucked good. And I trust this man, so I'm going to tell him.

"Give me the rest of my penance. Fuck me senseless till I scream," I say, then I thrust my hand between my thighs.

Gabe pounds me in a ruthless rhythm as I feverishly stroke myself till I'm caught up.

My orgasm crashes into me, over me, around me.

It pulls me under, and I shout incoherent cries of pleasure.

The world winks off, but as it spins away, Gabe's grunts and growls land in my ear, echo in my heart.

A few minutes later, when I look in the bathroom mirror, red marks bloom on my ass.

I smile.

Those marks are mine. My private marks from this man.

23

DOG KISSES

ELLIE

Can I go to bed now?

Because...wow.

After the sex, and then the shower—where he luxuriously washed my whole body, then rubbed lotion onto my bruised skin when we got out—I'm... utterly spent.

In the bathroom, he brings me a shirt. It's royal blue.

A very familiar color.

I take it from him, holding it up, turning it around. Number eighty-eight.

When I pull on his jersey, I'm swimming in it. "It's like a dress," I say, gesturing to where the hem hits my thigh.

"A damn sexy one," he says, and he pulls on boxer briefs. Nice snug black ones.

Then he scoops me up in his arms and carries me out of the spacious bathroom. "Where are you taking me?" I ask, laughing.

"Wherever you want to go, sweetheart," he says, but he's got a plan since he crosses the big bedroom, where I eye his king-size bed longingly, then brings me to the living room. Carefully, he sets me down on the plush, U-shaped gray couch. He sits next to me and rubs a hand along my thigh. "Stay the night," he says.

"Mmm. That sounds nice. You wore me out," I say on a yawn that I try to stifle.

"Good. You need your rest. Next week is a big one for you," he says.

It takes me a few seconds to connect the dots. Oh, right. Next week. Just the reason I'm here. Just the start of my new life in Los Angeles. When I work on set. When we have our first table read. When we prep to shoot the first episode of my show.

My show.

"I still can't believe it's happening," I say, a little giddy—maybe from the prospect of living my dreams, or maybe too from the afterglow of intense sex.

Or, possibly, a cocktail of the two.

"You deserve it," he says, then takes my hand in his and starts rubbing the space between my thumb and forefinger. "These hands will get sore from all that writing," he says. "Gotta take care of them."

Can you *take care of them*?

I moan into the pleasure of the hand rub as he kneads my palm. "Are you ready for Monday?" he asks.

My head is still in such a fog from sex, but I do my best to clear it. "Yes. I worked on the script today at Maddox's house. Made a few final tweaks. I kind of can't wait for the table read," I say.

He digs his thumb into the center of my palm, pressing hard. "Makes sense. That's how I always feel about training camp too. It's exhausting, but I love it too."

"Yes. Exactly. I know I'll be working crazy hours—probably round the clock—but this is something I've wanted for a long time now. I'm lucky to even have the chance to produce a show at all."

He scoffs. "It's not luck. It's talent, skill, hard work."

He's not wrong. But Hollywood relies a lot on luck too. "True, but making it in this business definitely takes some stardust and magic. When you find it, you can't let anything get in the way. This is a huge chance for me to prove to the whole damn world that I have what it takes to jump from being onscreen to being behind the cameras."

He brings my palm to his soft mouth. "And you

will," he says, then his gaze drifts to my necklace. "That's cute. Very you."

I finger the typewriter charm. "Thanks. I do like jewelry. I picked it up at Rachel's jewelry boutique tonight," I say, feeling better than I did when I last saw her. I can tell her about tonight, and I won't feel like I lied. I *did* open my heart to Gabe. "Oh! And I have dinner with her Sunday night at this place right near her shop. I basically commandeered her into being my new best friend."

He laughs. "I'm sure it was so hard for her to say yes to spending time with you," he says, then studies the charm a bit more. "Hold on, just a sec."

He rises, retreats to the bedroom, and returns with his fist closed, wrapped around something. When he sits back next to me on the couch, he opens it.

I squeal. "It's gorgeous! How can you not wear this every day? I would never take it off."

He laughs, then kisses my hair as I fondle his Super Bowl ring. Diamonds and sapphires gleam on the massive piece of jewelry. "It's like something a mafia boss would wear."

"Yeah, only it probably won't fit on your pinkie," he says.

"I'll stuff it with cotton or string or whatever and make it fit," I say, running my fingers along the etching with the number of the game, the name of his team. It's both gaudy and breathtaking. "I remember seeing you play in this game on TV," I say, flashing back to a few years ago. "That catch you made."

"Which one, sweetheart?" he asks, deservedly cocky. "I made a lot of catches in that game."

I gawk at the ring. "All of them."

Then, he takes it from my hand, like playtime is over. Except, it's not. Gently, he wiggles it onto my thumb.

It fits perfectly. My grin is bigger than the sky. "I love it."

"Looks good on you," he says, then his gaze travels down to my rear. "Are you sore?"

"Only in the best of ways."

He lifts up the hem of my shirt, whistling in admiration at the marks he left. "Glad we abandoned the picnic," he says, with a sly smile. "But are you still hungry?"

"I think that hummus might be calling my name. Maybe the pie. We didn't even break it open."

Like it's such a damn shame we took off early for our version of *church*.

"And the pie looked damn good," he says.

"I got it at this cute little bakery near me earlier today. When I was out walking—" I bolt up upright. I can't believe I forgot my love. "Shoot. I need to go."

"What's wrong?" he asks, a line digging into his forehead.

"Gigi has been alone for a few hours now," I say, then hustle around his living room, hunting for my clothes, my canvas bag, my purse. "How could I have nearly forgotten her? I mean, she can hold it for a long time—she's trained and everything. I just meant I can't stay the night."

He moves swiftly into action, jumping up from the couch to join me. "I'll get her," he says, setting a hand on my arm as I'm grabbing my phone from the table.

I jerk my gaze toward him, my hand freezing on the device. "What?"

He tucks a finger under my chin. "You're exhausted, baby. Stay here. Eat something. I'll get your dog and bring her back to spend the night too," he says. "If that's okay with you?"

If that's okay with me? Holy smokes. That's more than okay. That's next level. "You want to drive to my house, fetch my dog, and bring her here?"

His brow knits deeper. "Um, yeah," he says, like it's obvious that's the sequence.

And it is.

But wow.

Just wow.

"Okay," I say, feeling a little bubbly, then I give him the code to my garage and the keys to my car.

"Use my car though, because she has a dog seat in the back with a seat belt and everything."

Shaking his head in amusement, he says, "Of course she does."

Then he leaves, and I lie down on his couch, where I stare at the ring a little longer, feeling fizzy.

Feeling wanted.

I reach for my phone, open it, and type out a message to Rachel. *The date was amazing. Can't wait to tell you about it.*

I hit send, then I crack open a new book.

But before the heroine even bumps into the hot guy under a ladder, my eyes are floating closed, and I'm swimming off.

Someone is kissing me.

Someone is rubbing against me.

Someone is licking my mouth.

I stretch and open my eyes. Gigi is engaged in a full kiss attack. With a yawn, I push up on the couch, where I'm slathered in more canine love, whimpers, and *where have you beens.*

"I missed you too, girl," I murmur. Then my gaze swings to the tiled floor. What's that pink fluffy thing? A pillow? "Do you have shaggy pink couch cushions?" I ask, looking up at my man as he walks closer.

Gabe flops down on the couch next to me. "No. I got Gigi a dog bed for the night," he says.

Silly boy. She sleeps on the human bed. But the gesture sends my heart into overdrive.

This man made me a picnic. Picked up my dog. Bought her a bed. Bruised my body in all the best ways.

I need a way to stop time and live in this moment forever.

But I also need to fight off the inevitable heartache. We're on a honeymoon. It ends tomorrow night, then we return to reality. We will go our separate ways. He'll head to training camp and to the love of his life—football. I'll be working long days and long nights to build the next phase of my life. And I was fine with that when we first started. But now, I'm definitely not.

SATURDAY

A Day

24

———

I'VE GOT THIS

Ellie

We're five miles away from my mom's home when my phone trills. Mom's calling.

Of course.

"Want me to hit answer?" Gabe asks from the passenger seat as we cruise down a winding road in the town where we both grew up.

"Of course," I say, and he swipes up. I call out cheerily, "You're on speaker, Mama Snow. Gabe's here."

"Hello, Gabe, you cutie-pie," she says.

I snort-laugh.

He hisses at me, then says aloud in a chipper voice, "Hello, Mrs. Snow." I've never heard him use that voice with me. That must be the good-boy voice. The one that convinced the book club ladies he was a sweet, wholesome lad.

Ha ha.

"It's going to be such a treat to see you both. And," my mom says, then takes a pause, "do you mind popping into Trader Joe's and picking up an extra pink lemonade? It's a mile from where you are."

"Mom!"

"Sweetheart, you never turned off the sharing," she says, like this is all my fault.

Yup. I only have myself to blame. "Of course, Mom," I say, happy to help.

We make a quick pit stop and when we hop back into my car, a reminder flashes across my phone.

Email Sidney.

I can't put this off much longer. "That's the producer for *Fabio's List*," I explain to Gabe as I pull back onto the road to Mom's.

"Yeah? What did you decide?"

"I haven't decided yet," I say, but the second those words come out, they feel wrong.

Why am I hiding from *Fabio's List*?

The show is airing whether I say anything or not. I dated Dexter whether I appear on camera or not. I'll probably be named regardless. I can't hide from the doc, which has tongues wagging already. Might as well say my piece.

I lift my chin as I drive. "Actually, I *am* going to do it. So what if I dated a scam artist? I'm moving on into this new life here, bruises on my butt and all."

"Do they hurt?" he asks, looking at me.

I shake my head and turn on the blinker. "Nope. But I like knowing they're there."

"Mmm. Me too." He sounds happy—but romantic too. I catch him studying me as if he's hunting for something in my expression.

"What is it?" I ask curiously.

He shakes his head, but he's smiling now. "Just thinking." He says it like it's a good thing, with the same warm tone he takes when he's talking about *us*.

Bubbles of hope swim in my bloodstream. Has he been thinking *could there be more* too? Oh, god. Oh, wow. That's almost too much to consider.

"About what?" I ask, trying to mask the hope in my voice.

Gabe shrugs like he's holding in a secret. He's still grinning. "Just how fun this week was."

I fight off a goofy smile. "It was amazing."

"And you're pretty fired up right now," he says.

"I am," I say, desperate to add *because of you, because of that call, because of all these good things.*

Except driving isn't the time to tackle a Big Topic. Maybe later? After the party? We do have to return to Los Angeles tonight. Rachel's dog sitting Gigi this evening, and I need to swing by and pick up my girl.

But I could ask Gabe to spend one more night with me, then maybe ask for more...

But his smile burns off as he asks, "Because of the call?"

Huh. What? "What do you mean?" I ask.

"You're fired up because of that call," he clarifies.

Um. Yeah.

And maybe he wasn't thinking about *us*. Maybe he was just being a good guy, asking questions, showing an interest.

Stay grounded, Ellie. Take your time. You have the whole night. You have the drive home to sort through this storm of feelings.

I fight off my romantic fantasies and stick to brass tacks. "Absolutely, it was a great week, and I feel super relieved that I've decided what to do about *Fabio's List*. The interview's been weighing on me."

"Hmm," he murmurs, like he's weighing the interview too. I steal a quick glance at the passenger. His jaw is set tight, his gaze staring straight ahead. Something's on his mind, and I wish I knew what. Several seconds later, he says, "Got it. Makes sense. That was a big moment then with the whole... moving on."

"Yes," I say, relieved at last. Finally, we're on the same wavelength again. The one where we talk freely about work and the past and changes. The one where he understands what I'm trying to do with my life here in Los Angeles. Maybe this is a big moment for us too—where we connect over the way we understand each other. "And life's big moments call for songs."

He arches a brow, then like he's maybe resetting from a few seconds ago, he nods. "I'm down with that. So you want a tune to celebrate your whole new life here and all?"

Yes, he gets me. "That sounds perfect. But what about you? Do you have a celebration song?"

"Sure. When I score a touchdown at home, The Mercenaries play Stone Zenith's 'He's One Badass Dude.'"

I crack up. "You do know Stone wrote that about his husband?"

Gabe scoffs. "And his hubs *is* a badass dude. And so am I."

"Fair point."

Gabe pats the dashboard. "What's your tune? Let's blast it."

"Ten-Speed Rabbit's 'I Got This,'" I say. A great song by a fabulous English group.

"I don't know that song or the band," he says.

"Allow me to introduce you, then. The lead singer was my friend Veronica's first client, so I gotta support my girls. 'I Got This' is definitely my walk-up song. It's the ultimate girl-power tune." I point to my phone, excited to share something I love with him, like the bedtime story the other night. "Playlist two."

He hits the song. The lyrics blast through the air, lifting me higher. *Don't worry about me, Doing it my way, My girls and me, We've got a plan.*

He turns introspective.

"Sing with me," I urge as I rock out to the tune's epic chorus that my friends and I know by our karaoke hearts. *I've got this, I've got this.*

But he flashes me a brief smile, then returns to watching the houses pass by. I try to keep the mood upbeat, belting out the anthem as we go.

As the closing notes fade, we pull up to my parents' home. I feel energized again, from the song, from the conversation, from the possibility of talking to him tonight. On the ride home perhaps. Or maybe at my house. I'll use this time at the party to sift through my feelings and figure out what to say exactly.

When I cut the engine, I stare at the two-story white house with green shutters and planters bursting with flowers.

Whoa.

Butterflies flap in my chest then crawl up my throat.

I'm going into my childhood home with the guy down the street. This is so surreal. This was my high school fantasy.

Now it's my reality. But...not really. It's still just a dating challenge until I tell him my heart.

I don't want to play this game anymore.

I resolve to be real. To be truly vulnerable once again. And why wait till the end of the night? I could say something right now. Tell him I don't want to go our separate ways.

I turn to him. "Gabe—"

But he's already leaning across the console, brushing a chaste kiss to my cheek, shutting me up. "It's our last night. We've been practicing all week. Like the song says, you've got this," he says, then pats the dashboard and jumps out of the car.

Resolute.

Confident.

He's a badass dude strutting away from scoring a touchdown, ready for the next play.

When all I can hear is *Last night, last night, last night.*

Everything I was going to say lodges in my throat as he comes around to the driver's side and opens my door.

I step out, bewildered and off-balance.

Was that heavy-handed reminder necessary? And in that cocky tone too.

Grabbing the gift I bought for Aunt Tilly from the back seat, along with the lemonade for Mom, I head up the steps, aching everywhere.

I was foolishly hoping he might want more too.

But this was only ever a fling.

When my mom sweeps open the door, I give her a big and necessary hug. It's good to be home. It's good to see her especially as I hold back the knot of emotions in my throat.

25

CROQUET OOMPH

Gabe

This sucks.

I nurse a cup of pink lemonade and tap a purple ball with a wooden mallet.

The ball rolls painfully slowly as my dad, alongside Ellie's, flips beef and veggie burgers on the grill.

My mom chuckles then shakes her head. "Gabe, hon, you have to hit it harder."

"Surely, you can put some more oomph into lawn croquet," Ellie's mom encourages.

"Normally, you're such a pro at this," Tilly weighs in.

Gee. Anyone else want to comment on my shitty technique?

I don't need advice. I know the reason for my poor performance. I've been distracted by my sullen mood.

It's not Mom's fault. Or Mrs. Snow's. Or Tilly's.

Hell, it's hardly Ellie's fault.

It's fucking fate's fault.

Nope. That's wrong. It's my fault.

I can't even fashion a smart comeback. Instead, I mutter, "Thanks for the tips." I head to the purple ball, which is next to Ellie. She smells like cherry blossoms. That sucks too.

She smells too wonderful. Too much like my future.

But she's not mine. Hell, she never was. And tonight she's simply my...fake date?

Fuck. I don't even know what she is anymore, except...*she's moving on.*

That I know for sure. She's made that abundantly clear in the last twenty-four hours. She is an independent woman, and she needs no man.

Just as I was gearing up to maybe ask if she wanted to make a go of things after training camp, to date for real when I return...Boom.

She drops the mic on her whole boss-lady-moving-on soliloquy.

More power to her and blah, blah, blah. But there's no room for romance in her work-all-day/be-single-all-night plans.

That song she blasted was an exclamation point punctuating her speech about business and new life stages and moving the fuck on.

"Ooh! Look at that one!" Tilly hoots. I blink, then reconnect with the game in time to see her green ball roll through an arch as she makes her shot.

"You go, Aunt Tilly!" Ellie shouts, then she nudges me, giving me a bright smile. "Good one, right?"

"Yeah, great," I mutter.

She tilts her head, looks at me, clearly worried. "Are you okay?" she whispers. She sounds just like a girlfriend when her boyfriend's being a moody jerk at a party.

Well, the last part *is* true.

"I'm fine," I mumble, but I can't shake my attitude.

"You don't seem like yourself," she says, trying again in a low voice.

"I'm fine," I repeat.

She tugs gently on my forearm, guiding me away from the game, toward the side of the yard. I follow her because of course I follow her. I'd fucking follow her anywhere. And that's the goddamn problem.

I'd chase her, I'd beg her, I'd go wherever she went.

I'm crazy for her, but she's already gone, belting

out *I don't need anyone* songs and celebrating her romance-free life.

And I can't, I just fucking can't, ruin shit for her by telling her I fell for her in *only* four nights.

I can't stand to hear her say, *Oh Gabe, that's nice and all, but I came to Los Angeles to be free.*

So here at the edge of the lawn, I just stare past her.

She tries to catch my eye, angling her chin just so, to get me to look at her. "Are you sure? Because you don't seem okay."

Gritting my teeth, I shovel a hand through my hair. I feel like a bomb's ticking in my chest.

No, Ellie, I'm not okay. I'm not okay at all because I want to break our deal in spectacular fashion. I want to take you into my arms and smother you in kisses and keep you for all the nights.

But you want to just...move on.

And if I stay outside at the party with her, I'll blurt out all these painful feelings that are clawing at me.

Feelings that she doesn't have the time or space for.

I thrust my mallet at her, and she takes it automatically. "Sorry, sweetheart. My agent called earlier, and I've got some stuff on my mind about the football season. It's nothing. But I'm going to take a walk and clear my head."

She frowns. "Oh." Then she clears her expression, putting on a small smile. She's a good actress, but I'm pretty sure it's fake—like this whole week has been. "I'll be here," she says.

I can barely hear her because I'm already walking away.

* * *

Thirty minutes later, I'm a little less annoyed thanks to some air and a walk, but I'm not any happier. Hell, I'm both sadder and angrier, mostly at myself for falling for a woman who's so clearly unavailable.

Who *told me* she was unavailable.

But my stew of feelings doesn't matter. This is not my birthday. This is not my party. I need to get my act together so I can handle the rest of the night.

When I trudge up the steps to Ellie's parents' home and push open the door, I catch sight of Ellie pacing in the kitchen, phone pressed to her ear, her back to me.

"Great. Email me the details," she says.

There's a pause.

"Yes, Sidney, I think it can help other women learn from my experiences too," she says.

She's talking to the producer of that documentary about her ex, and my frustration ramps up again.

Then she says goodbye and turns down the hall. "I said yes to the interview, Mom."

Like James Bond, I creep across the hardwood and listen in to her private conversation with her mother. It's like sticking my finger in a fire, but I do it anyway. I need to know where she's at. I want to be certain that my instincts in the car were right.

"Are you sure, sweetie?"

"Absolutely. I was just protecting myself when they first called. Not dealing with the past. But this is how I can put it behind me. That's what I've been trying to figure out this past week. How to put it behind me. And this will give me some closure."

"Then I support you," her mom says.

"Thanks, Mom. These last few days have given me a lot of clarity."

That seals the deal. This last week was everything we'd agreed it would be—a week and nothing more. I'm the fool who got caught up in her.

I close my eyes and slump down.

* * *

Somehow, I make it through the rest of the evening. But when the party winds down, and Ellie's grabbing her things to leave, she pulls me aside by the front door.

"Hey. You don't seem like yourself," she says quietly, then she adds, "Maybe we can talk on the way home?"

Her voice rises with hope.

But no fucking way.

I can't be alone with her in the car when she breaks my heart again.

Like I'm on the field, and I've been swarmed by the secondary and have to scramble to get away, I think on my feet. *Fast.*

With a big, fat yawn, I say, "I'm exhausted. I'm going to crash at my parents' house. But hey, this was fun. Glad you got to take your good guy challenge this week. Glad it worked out for you."

I drop a careful kiss to her forehead, and I get the hell out of there before she can slice off another piece of my heart.

SUNDAY

No Caramel Lattes for You. Or Pancakes Either.

26

MY BIG CHANCE

Ellie

The people-watching at Edge & Plow on the main drag in Venice is top-notch on a Sunday morning. I enjoy the view from an outside table, sipping a cup of tea, my pup in my lap.

Over there, a gal my age sporting a messy bun and cut-off shorts shows pics—I presume—on her phone to her friends. They're all dressed in the ragtag attire of a morning-after post-mortem.

My heart clutches and I look away.

A few tables over from me, a man with a neat beard excitedly tells his buddies all about last night with *like, the sexiest guy ever.*

Good for him, but I frown.

There could not be a more inspiring scene for my writing soul. This is the kind of background I could see in an episode of *The Dating Games*.

And yet, I'm too sad.

I'm alone. I'm not here with my New York girlfriends. Veronica has returned to Manhattan with Milo. Hazel has taken off for Europe.

I'm not here with my Los Angeles friends either.

I lift my black tea—because I can't indulge in caramel iced lattes every day—take a sip, then set the cup on the iron table.

Even if Maddox or Rachel were here, what would I say? The guy I was falling for just walked away from me.

I heave a sigh, shoulders slumped. Gigi looks up, concern in her big eyes as her ears go to full bat-style.

My throat tightens and I stroke her soft head. "Of course, you're my friend too," I tell her. She leans into my hand, savoring the pets.

Then, I finish the tea, bus my table, and leave. I walk my girl to our new home, trying desperately to look forward to tomorrow.

To my big day, my big week, my big chance.

But it's harder than it was less than a week ago when I pulled into town.

27

—————

IT WAS OBVIOUS

Gabe

As I towel off from the shower, the scent of eggs and pancakes floats up the stairs of my parents' house and wafts into the bathroom.

Damn, I've missed the smell of Dad's cooking. Smells like home.

I dry off and then track down the pair of gym shorts and fresh T-shirt I left behind last time I spent the night in my old bedroom, aka the *guest room*. Still feels like mine even though it's done up in pretty whites and blues now—gender neutral for guests, Mom says—and it no longer has any posters of my sports idols or favorite rock stars on the wall.

Shame.

I pad downstairs, determined to put yesterday out of mind. That's a skill I've honed from decades as an athlete. Mental skills were always my thing way back in high school. I could block out the world. I damn well plan to do that now.

When I reach the kitchen, Dad is plating some scrambled eggs and pancakes. The welcoming aroma of fresh coffee curls through the air.

Yeah, this might help me forget Ellie too. C'mon, coffee. Work your magic.

"Smells delish, Dad," I say.

He flashes me a smile. "Thanks. I hope your mom likes it. She should be back from her morning walk in a few minutes."

I furrow my brow. "Wait. I don't get any?"

He chuckles, setting a hand on his belly. "You thought this was for you?"

Well, yeah. "Um, I was hoping so," I say sheepishly.

He arches a salt-and-pepper eyebrow. "After the way you acted last night?"

I flinch. "What?"

Dad shoots me a *you can't fool me kid* stare. "Gabe," he chides.

I shrug helplessly as I lean against the kitchen counter. "I have no idea what you're talking about."

He turns the heat down on the stove. "You were kind of a dick at Tilly's party."

I snap my gaze to him, lips parting in protest. "I was not," I say. But I know that's a bald-faced lie. From his look, Dad didn't buy it either.

I sigh heavily. "Shit. It was that obvious?"

He nods once. "You kind of huffed and puffed your way around the place."

I drag a hand over my chin. "Did Tilly notice?"

"I hope not. But I bet Ellie did. Seemed she was the one you were a jerk to."

Does he have X-ray vision? "How did you know?"

He laughs, eyes rolling. "Gabe, when you played croquet, you were all broody-faced," he says, adopting a sour expression.

I wince, knowing he's right.

"And then later, you were just kind of..." He pauses, perhaps to search for words, and I catch the sound of the front door before he finishes, "Short. Clipped."

I drop my head into my hand, covering my face in embarrassment. "That's bad."

"What's bad?"

I look up at the question as my mom comes in. She's not alone. She's with Ellie's aunt Tilly. Of course. The two ladies are morning walking partners.

I waste no time with justifications. Dad was right. "I'm sorry I was a moody jerk last night," I tell the guest of honor.

Tilly tilts her head, her gaze unsure. "About our

croquet tips?" she asks, then laughs, patting my shoulder. "Don't worry. We love trash talking you. It's too fun to beat up on a pro baller."

I smile, digging her easygoing style. Her quick forgiveness. She's like Ellie—warm and inviting.

The mere thought of Ellie tugs on my heart, but I've got to fix what I messed up with my family before anything else.

"No, Tilly. I mean, I was kind of pissy all night at your party," I say, then quickly correct myself. "I wasn't kind of pissy. I just was moody, and that's not cool. I'm sorry."

She squeezes my arm. "It's fine, sweetie. We can't be perfect all the time. I barely even noticed."

I'm grateful for the reprieve, but this is only the start. I turn to my mother. "Sorry, Mom. I should have done better."

"It happens." She smiles sympathetically. "I'm guessing you had woman trouble?"

I blink. What is it with my parents seeing right through me? I scrub a hand along my scratchy jaw. "I don't know," I mutter.

"Sounds like woman trouble, then," my dad says sagely. Then he nudges the plate toward my mom. "Eat up before it gets cold, hon." Dad glances at Tilly. "Want some too?"

"You're a doll," Tilly says brightly.

"Did I luck out or what? I married a man who feeds me *and* my friends," Mom says.

Dad makes another plate, and the ladies sit at the kitchen counter and tuck in. My stomach growls, and I stare forlornly at the emptying pan. There are hardly any eggs left. No pancakes either.

But that's okay. I glance over at my pops, the one who taught me to cook. He doesn't have a plate either.

"Dad, you want some? I can make some for us both," I offer.

He smiles proudly, as if I finally understood an assignment. "I'd love some."

Then I whip up a fresh batch of eggs and pancakes. At least I fixed one problem. Too bad I can't solve the problem of bad timing with Ellie Snow as easily.

But maybe I should start with something I *can* do. I need to apologize to her for how I acted last night. I can't let her think I'm that kind of guy.

* * *

Later, when I'm back home after a big team meeting, I pack for training camp and contemplate the best way to say, *Sorry, I was a jerk.*

I toss a few more T-shirts into my duffel bag, still

mulling over the question, then there's a knock on my door.

My heart springs. Maybe it's Ellie.

I hustle over and answer. On the doorstep stands Myrtle, my neighbor. I'm bummed it's not Ellie, but I'm always happy to see my neighbor. "Hi, Myrtle."

"Hey, handsome. Any chance you could help me put my suitcase away?"

"Of course," I say. "Happy to help."

I shut the door and follow her to her condo. "How was the retreat?" I ask, and maybe it's weird that I'm asking the little old lady down the hall about her kink workshop. But, you know, maybe it's not either.

"Oh, it was enlightening. I learned so much," she says as we wander through her home. "New techniques. New preferences. The world is changing. Playmates like different things these days, and I need to be able to deliver for my subs."

Holy Shit. Myrtle's a Dom. That's...badass boss lady.

"That's awesome," I say, grinning.

In her bedroom, she gestures to her empty suitcase. I hoist it up and set it on the top shelf.

Then, I dust my hands and meet her gaze. Her blue eyes are wise, crinkled at the corners, like she knows things.

Not just things about kink—things about life, and how to behave, and how to say you're sorry.

"Hey, Myrtle. Can I ask your advice on something?"

"Of course, handsome."

"There's this woman," I begin, then I lay it all out.

When I'm done telling her the story of Ellie, she just laughs. "Young people," she says, shaking her head.

"What does that mean?"

"Sometimes you miss all the clues," she says.

Myrtle waves me over to the kitchen counter. "Have a cup of coffee while I tell you everything you got wrong and how to make it right."

As we chat, I thumb through the mental Instagram of my week with Ellie.

I got all these good, romantic, hopeful vibes from her and then suddenly, she was all Miss Independent before the party.

The last thing I wanted when we stopped at her house was for her to turn to me with that decisive expression and tell me she just wanted to be friends or whatever, so I interrupted her.

But she wasn't about to go all *I've got this* on me. She was, maybe, possibly, about to tell me she felt the same way I do.

Fuck me.

I missed what was right in front of me.

28

IS THIS SEAT TAKEN?

Ellie

"And then she said, I'll take ten of those heart necklaces," Rachel says, setting down her wine glass at the bar, triumphantly.

Delighted with her tale of saleswomanship, I raise my glass to my new friend.

Then my old friend joins in. Maddox is here too, at Max's Restaurant. He was finishing dinner with a client, so I insisted he join us for a post-dinner drink.

Already, the three of us are thick as thieves, sitting around a high table near the bar.

Maddox lifts his tumbler of amber liquid. "To being a helluva dealmaker," he says to Rachel.

I stretch across to pat his forearm. "And this guy

knows how to ink all the deals. He's the best in the biz," I say, proudly.

He waves off the compliment, then directs his attention to Rachel. "Tell me more about the boutique and what inspired you to open it," he says.

I sit back, enjoying the camaraderie as I get to know Rachel even better. She's not a replacement for my New York friends. She's her own woman, and I'm glad I have her in my life now.

I'm glad I have Maddox too.

Like in my TV show, friends make everything better. Friends, too, can help you through heartache.

When Rachel is done telling the story, her brown eyes meet mine in a question. "So, your date...how did it go? You've been holding out all night."

"Yes, inquiring minds want to know," Maddox seconds.

My poor heart hurts too much. But keeping the story to myself won't help me heal. "I reconnected with this guy, and we made a deal to spend the week together," I say as Rachel leans forward, while Maddox squints off in the distance. Weird. He's usually such a good listener, but everyone has their off days. "We had an amazing time over the last week, and I thought we were both feeling the spark of something more, but then—"

"Excuse me. Is this seat taken?"

I sit up straighter, my eyes widening at the smoky, sexy voice coming from behind me.

This can't be happening. A curl of pleasure winds down my spine. And I risk a glance over my shoulder.

My breath catches at the sight of the man I'm crazy for. His hands are wrapped around the back of the empty seat.

Like we mapped out on text with opening lines and all.

My heart climbs up my throat. *This has to be good. Please let this be good.*

"Now it is," I say, giving him the next line for our strangers-at-a-bar scenario.

But this role play is just between us, so I turn to my friends. "I'll be fine," I tell them. "You can go."

Rachel pushes back in her stool, grinning like *you'd better tell me everything.* Maddox squeezes my shoulder, then mouths *tomorrow* as he stands to go.

In seconds they're gone, and Gabe sits next to me. "I saw you here and I was compelled to come over and talk to you, even though I don't know you," he says, leaning into the role play.

Normally, I've led the scenes, improvising with him following. This time, I let him tell the story. I'm still hurting over last night, but I'm also delighted that he's here.

"What did you want to talk about?" I ask, carefully.

He might just be here for more sex. He might just be here to strike an arrangement.

He blows out a deep breath. "There's this guy I know," he begins. "He was such a dick last night, and he needs to apologize to his woman."

My heart jumps, but does that mean he still wants me to be *his*?

"Does he, now?" I ask, hunting for the answer in his eyes.

His dark brown eyes are vulnerable. "He was moody and cold, and he handled everything badly. And that's not cool," he says, but then he winces, drags a hand over his chin. "Shit, Ellie. I'm sorry. I can't do it like this."

"Like what?" I ask, alarmed that he's backing off. Is he saying he thought he could make a go of things but now he can't?

He lifts a hand, cups my cheek. "I'm crazy for you. Just absolutely crazy for you, and I want you to be mine. No games, no challenges, no fake dates. All real, if you'll have me," he says, taking the narrative for himself and leaving the stranger play far behind.

My lips tremble, and I'm overjoyed. By the simplicity, by the honesty, by the complete break of character. "I'm pretty wild for you too. For real," I say, then lift my chin in a request for a kiss.

He obliges, brushing his lips across mine with a sigh. "Fuck, baby. I fell so hard for you. I was terrified you didn't want the same things I did."

Melting in his arms, I swat his broad chest. "You're ridiculous. Of course I do," I say.

"I had no idea. You're all *I've got this* and shit, and I thought there was no room for me in your life."

"I thought there was no room for me in *your* life! Your last football season and all," I point out, and we're both laughing and smiling and touching.

"I want to spend my last season with you. And then whatever comes after that," he says.

I'm floating, and I can't be in public with him much longer. "Me too," I say, then I kiss him—a tender, passionate kiss that feels like a promise.

When we break it, I say, "Hey, stranger, I better pay this bill and take you home. I have something in mind for tonight."

"Tell me," he says urgently.

"I'll show you."

A minute later, we're gone.

29

NEW NECKLACE

Gabe

She shows me all right.

There's no scene, though. Just my woman riding me. Her palms press hard against my chest, her hips swivel, and her breath comes hot and fast. Her expression twists in exquisite pleasure, and she's close.

She's so damn close.

I slide a hand between her thighs. Stroke her till she's shaking. "So good," she murmurs.

"Because it's you and me, baby," I tell her as my other hand snakes up to her hair, curls around her head.

We can play all the bedroom games we want. We

can take on all the roles that suit us. We can go dirty and wild every night, but there's only one reason it feels this good.

Because we belong together.

As her orgasm crashes over her, mine follows, taking me under and into this bliss.

After, I pull her close, kiss her tenderly. Then I brush her hair off her face. "I'm falling in love with you, sweetheart."

She smiles. "I'm falling in love with you."

Later, after we clean up, we return to bed together. In seconds, the dog hops up, sliding between us. "Gigi," I chide.

Ellie laughs. "Gabe, there's something I have to tell you."

"Yeah, what's that?" I ask, on a yawn, content with the world.

"She doesn't sleep on dog beds. She sleeps with me."

I curl an arm around woman and dog. "You mean with *us*," I correct her.

Ellie snuggles up against us and we fall asleep like that.

In the morning, I'm out of bed at the crack of dawn. I take Gigi for her walk, then return to Ellie's home, where she's padding softly out of her bedroom, stretching.

"I need to get ready for the first day at work," she says.

"And I need to take off." I look at the clock on the wall. "Training camp check-in is at two."

Her eyes pop. "And it's in San Diego. You better go," she says, shooing me toward the door.

But not so fast. There's one thing I have to give her before I leave. I reach into my pocket for a little white cloth bag. Myrtle gave it to me to use, reminding me a man shouldn't apologize empty-handed.

"I have a little something for you," I say, then hand Ellie the bag.

She peers inside and brightens. "I love jewelry."

"I know," I say, then I fasten the chain around her neck. My Super Bowl ring dangles on the end of it. "Looks like that's exactly where it was meant to be."

30

MATCHMAKER

Gabe

A Few weeks later

Best training camp ever. The guys are sharp. The rookies don't act like privileged jackasses. Coach has me work closely with a couple of the new receivers and they learn the routes quickly, then play tight, intense football.

The way it should be.

By the end of training camp, we already feel like a well-oiled machine.

As I head off the grass on our final day at the San Diego facility, Coach calls me over. "Clements, nice job the last few weeks. I appreciate you stepping it up to help the kids."

"Happy to do it."

"You bring focus and talent and you give one hundred percent to every game."

"That's what the game deserves," I say. No point in playing half-assed. Ever.

"Are you sure this is your last season?" he asks, with a hopeful note in his voice.

I laugh. I had a feeling he was buttering me up for something—in this case, to get me to stay beyond my last year. "I'm pretty sure."

"But you've hardly had any injuries your whole career," he says, in a leading the witness tone. "And you're looking sturdy and fast as a fox."

I peer around, hunting for wood to knock, but of course finding none. "That's how I'd like to go out, sir. Injury free."

He nods, exhaling deeply, perhaps in understanding. "Fair enough. Just glad we've got you for the last season."

"Me too."

I trot the rest of the way off the field, catching up with Drew in the corridor. "That was a great training camp," I remark.

"What a difference a year makes," he seconds. Last year at this time, he was still playing on the Los

Angeles Devil Sharks. The Mercenaries traded for him right around the same time they traded for me.

"But I sure won't miss seeing you for the next few days," I add as we near the locker room.

He laughs. "Fucking won't miss seeing you either."

"Don't break the speed limit on your rush back to LA," I joke.

"Same to you," he says. And it's unsaid, but understood, why we're both eager to return to Los Angeles. He'll want to see his fiancée, Brooke, and I'm climbing the walls to see Ellie.

* * *

A little later, I'm heading to my car in the parking lot at the same time he is. Even though I don't want to waste a second before I see my woman, I also want to do something for her. I clear my throat. "So you want to grab a bite sometime when we're back in LA? You and Brooke and Ellie and me?"

As Drew tosses the keys to his Tesla up and down in his palm, he shoots me a cocky grin. "Aww. I thought you didn't want to see me and now you do."

I roll my eyes. "It's for Ellie, asshole. I know Ellie would like to meet Brooke. And I bet they'd hit if off."

Drew doesn't give me shit this time when he says,

"She will. Brooke's awesome and so is Ellie. Let's do it."

Three hours later, I'm pulling up to Ellie's place. Before I even cut the engine, the front door flies open and my brunette beauty rushes across the lawn and out to the driveway. My heart soars, right along with my dick. Package deal, those two.

I step out of the car and close the distance in a heartbeat, hauling her into my arms. Right where she belongs. "I missed you," she says.

"You have no idea how much I missed you," I say, savoring the smell of her, the feel of her.

We head inside. Where someone else, evidently, missed me too. In the front hallway, Gigi does the dog greeting dance, jumping up and down, shouting my name in Dog. So I pick her up and kiss her little nose.

"You are the cutest," Ellie says.

Then I set down the little lady, and I spend a good long time kissing the woman I missed. The woman who was my fake real girlfriend. Now she's mine for always and that's exactly what I want.

Later, after we reconnect properly—or improperly as the case may be since Ellie turned out to be a very naughty student and I had to put her over my knee as her professor—we pore over dinner options in the kitchen. Once we choose Korean, I ask her if she wants to go out with Drew and Brooke sometime.

She lights up. "I would love that."

I drop a kiss to her forehead. "I had a feeling you would. I know you said you wanted to make friends in LA, and I think you and Brooke would get along."

"Look at you! You're like a friend matchmaker."

"I just want to make you happy," I tell her.

She smiles. "News flash. You do."

31

A COUPLE OF WORD DEVOURERS

Ellie

A few days later, on Sunday morning, Gabe and I walk along Ocean Avenue in Santa Monica, savoring the late summer sun as we make our way to The Tree House.

I squeeze his hand tighter. "It's kind of wild that I've only been in town for a month and we're already doing this," I muse.

"Having brunch on a Sunday," he says. "Just like everyone else."

"Nobody would know what we did last night," I tease.

"Not a single soul has any idea," he says in a dirty whisper.

We went to a hotel along the beach. We met at the bar. I was a businesswoman in town for a conference. He happened to be going to the same conference but had to catch a late flight back to New York. We didn't know each other. But he still had his hotel room for another hour, so he took me back to his room, tied my wrists with his tie, then bent me over the edge of the bed. Stranger sex with the man you're crazy for is absolutely fantastic.

But I put it out of my mind as we head into the cute café, looking for his friends.

Gabe nods toward the booth in the corner. "There they are," he says, a touch of excitement in his gravelly voice. It's sweet how he wants to do this for me.

As we head toward the table, bits of their conversation drift into my ears. Brooke and Drew are debating—from the sound of it—what baseball flick to watch that afternoon.

I smile when we arrive. "Hey there. I'm Ellie."

"Hey Ellie. So good to meet you," Brooke says warmly, then pops up to give me a hug.

I like her already. "I'm so excited to meet you."

After Gabe makes quick intros to Drew, we sit down and I slide right into the conversation. "So the debate is *Sweet Spot*, *Ace* and what was the other movie?"

Drew clears his throat. "*High and Tight*," he says

in a serious tone.

My spidey senses tingle. I arch a brow. "*High and Tight*? I feel like that's a trick name," I say and Brooke cracks up.

Drew laughs too. "I made it up," Drew says, with a casual shrug. "But it sounds plausible."

Gabe shakes his head in amusement, then stage whispers. "He's such a clown."

Brooke nods in agreement. "Drew is the biggest clown," she says.

"Also, I think *High and Tight's* probably a different kind of movie," I offer.

Brooke laughs, then adds, "Maybe not such a bad one either."

"Oh, we're going to get along well," I say to Brooke. I rub my palms. "All right. I have my vote on what movie you should watch."

Brooke beckons with her fingers. "Lay it on us."

"*Sweet Spot*," I declare.

Brooke's brown eyes light up. "Yes, because it's–"

"Based on a book," Brooke and I say in unison.

Then I shoo Drew away from his spot, so I can switch with him. "Move, I need to sit next to your fiancée. I've already decided she's fabulous and I adore her."

Brooke smiles. "I adore you too."

"And we need to talk about this book right now," I

add as we switch seats. With a harrumph, Drew takes my seat, but I don't think he's really mad.

"Yes we do," she says.

"Told you so," Gabe says to Drew.

"Yup. They like each other," Drew replies.

I smile, then I focus on Brooke. We spend most of the meal discussing our favorite books.

When we're done with the meal, the four of us wander through Santa Monica, the guys chatting about their next poker game, Axel's whereabouts, and who's looking strong on the pro basketball team.

With the guys a few steps behind us, Brooke shares insider tips with me on Venice, from the best bookstores to the best shops, since she's lived in that neighborhood for some time. "Bling and Baubles is my favorite. My friend Rachel owns that shop," she says offhand.

My jaw drops. "Wait. Jewelry shop Rachel is your friend too?" I ask in excitement.

"Yes. I've known her for a while."

"I already adopted her," I say, then tell Brooke how I met Rachel.

"Then that's perfect. Do you want to join us for ping-pong later this week?" Brooke asks.

I want nothing more than to play ping-pong with new friends. "I think this is the beginning of a beautiful friendship," I say.

"Me too," Brooke seconds.

I love LA.

32

———

MY CHEERLEADER

Gabe

First game of the season, and I am pumped. In the locker room before kickoff, the energy is bright and noisy.

Coach comes in and gives a no-nonsense *this is our time to show what focus is* speech.

When he's done, I smack palms with most of the guys, another one of our pre-game rituals. Then, when it's time to hit the field, our running back, Rand, chimes in with *let's go,* whooping and clapping as we trot out.

I've got my helmet in one hand, and my hacky sacks in the other.

Well, rituals matter and this is my streak ritual.

"Let's put these to use all season," I say to Drew as we reach the mouth of the tunnel.

He offers a fist for knocking. "You know we will."

Then, the announcer calls my name and number, and I run out on the field, Drew following shortly behind, as the last one, since he's the quarterback.

And when we win the coin toss, he's fast and lasered in on the target—*me*. I connect on the first pass of the opening drive, then gain another twenty-two yards.

A few plays later, I put it in the end zone.

And like that, we set a rhythm for the game. When I jog to the sidelines as special teams comes on, I look to the stands.

And I grin. There she is. At least, I think it's Ellie. We've got a packed crowd here.

But I snagged her seats on the fifty-yard line. I squint, just making her out next to Rachel and Maddox, I think. Brooke is here too since she's part of their crew now, and Ellie's become fast friends with her.

That's my woman. She knows how to get along with anyone—she's outgoing, friendly and unafraid.

But the real way I can tell it's Ellie is the outfit. She's wearing a cheerleader costume. A tiny, pleated skirt, a cute sweater, and a pair of pom-poms.

Well, later we have to role play naughty cheerleader and dirty football player.

I wave to her, then blow her a kiss.

When the game ends, I kiss her again, in the stands.

Then in the corridor.

Then at home, where she's the naughtiest cheerleader there ever is.

And to think I was determined to focus only on football this season. But I like playing ball even better when I have Ellie to come home to.

EPILOGUE

A Month or So Later

Ellie

One night in the fall, when Brooke's out of town for work, I meet Rachel and Maddox for dinner and ping-pong. It's the night of the *Fabio's List* premiere. We don't watch it. I don't want to watch it.

It's part of my past, and I'm perfectly fine with that. I did, however, already see my interview. The producer sent me an advance clip.

It was short and simple, and the segment was titled *Moving On.* "I credit my friends with helping me. They were there for me, and they helped me to see the signs. I'm grateful for them, and now I've fully moved on. I'm with a great guy," I'd said.

"What's he like?" the producer asked off camera.

"He's the ultimate good guy," I said with a smile.

Gabe is a good one, through and through. But at night, he's very, very bad. And that's just the way I like it.

I head to the ping-pong table and catch up with my friends, where Maddox tells us the latest on his love life.

Well, not everything. He's a private guy. But suffice to say, I'm eager for any details he'll share.

* * *

I settle onto my couch with my guy and my dog and a bowl of popcorn. It's been months and months of hard work and long hours and chewed nails, but it's finally time.

It's premiere night for *The Dating Games*.

The opening credits roll and when *Created by Ellie Snow* scrolls across the screen, Gabe hoots and hollers.

"That's my woman," he says, then smacks a kiss onto my cheek.

I'm lit up like fireworks as the show begins. It's surreal watching it on screen, knowing others are watching it too.

The next day, I find out just how many.

I believe the proper measurement is *a fuck ton.*

Enough that once the ten-episode season ends a little later, Webflix renews it.

But I'm not the only one having a good fall. In December, I round up my friends to head to the Mercenaries stadium, where we watch my boyfriend catch two touchdowns and nail a playoff spot.

He's celebrating on the field, but then he runs over to the sidelines, hoists me over the stands and onto the field, and kisses me madly.

"You made this the best season ever. I love you," he says, quiet but loud enough for me to hear above the noise of the crowd.

"I love you too," I say, so damn glad I took the good guy challenge for this great man.

FINAL EPILOGUE

Ellie

All the stockings are hung by the chimney with care. I adjust one over the mantel, liking the way it looks in my home. Well, it's almost our home now since Gabe is here nearly every night. Gigi stretches her legs behind her on the couch, posing frog style, the cutie. I walk over, since I can't resist giving her a little chin scratch. "It looks good, don't you think?"

It looks fabulous like it always does, I imagine she says.

A few presents sit under a little Christmas tree in the corner of the living room. Most are for Gigi since she loves her stuffed toys. Killing them that is.

Gabe and I decided to donate to each other's

favorite charities as gifts. He picked animal rescue for me, and I picked youth sports for him.

I savor the holiday view for another few seconds, until the sound of his shoes clicking across the floor grows louder. He must have just finished getting ready for the holiday party. He had a practice that ran late.

"Hey sweetheart. You ready?" he calls out.

I turn around and...wow. My guy is looking sharp and sexy in trim jeans and a dark blue button-down shirt. His stubble is working its magic on my libido.

But then again, Gabe works his magic on my libido all the time.

When his gaze meets mine, he stops in his tracks. His eyes roam up and down my body as he whistles in appreciation. "Damn woman," he says.

I smile at him, pleased he likes what he sees. "Glad you approve," I say, jutting out my hip. I'm wearing a simple red dress.

The dress isn't racy. It isn't showy. But I feel good in it, especially with his gaze on me.

"It's a wonder I kept my hands off you at that first eggnog party," he says, closing the distance and putting those fantastic hands all over me, curling them around my hips, sliding up my sides, then around my back.

"Well wonders can cease tonight," I say. Then I

give him a kiss, and when we separate, I say goodnight to Gigi.

My little lady curls up on her the pink dog bed Gabe gave her as we leave. We take off, hopping into my red convertible, to make our way to Aunt Tilly's eggnog party.

Once we head inside my aunt's pretty home, my mom sails over to us. She gives me a quick hug then turns immediately to the man by my side. "Gabe! I always knew you were the one for her," she says.

"You're a smart woman, Mrs. Snow. And I completely agree with you."

She pats Gabe on the shoulder. "I knew my Ellie would break the bad boy habit."

I grin privately. "I sure did."

Gabe's father strides over to us next, embracing his son. This isn't the first time we've seen my mom or Gabe's dad, but it always warms my heart to see Gabe and his father together. He has such a good relationship with his dad and it's lovely to watch the two of them. After we make small talk for a little bit, his dad asks him, "Pancakes tomorrow? Will you be staying the night?"

Gabe shakes his head apologetically. "Can't. We weren't able to get a sitter for Gigi tonight."

His dad chuckles almost under his breath. "You talk like you have kids."

Gabe's all serious when he says, "Well, she's ours so we have to look out for her."

His dad smiles. "All right. I get it."

We make the rounds, chatting with family and friends as the night unfolds, enjoying this party together, side by side. But later, as we grab our things to go, we walk under the mistletoe. In a flash, Gabe tugs me against him.

"Just like that night," he murmurs.

"I have such fond memories of that night," I say.

"I hope you have fond memories of this one too," he says, sounding a touch vulnerable.

"I do," I say, feeling warm and bubbly with him. "And I also think we happened at just the right time."

With a sexy rumble, he says, "Me too, sweetheart."

Then he kisses me under the mistletoe. My knees go weak. My belly flips. This man does it for me.

* * *

When we return to my place, he unlocks the door, but he seems a little distracted. That's not like him. He's usually relaxed, cool, in charge. He's borderline antsy now. Maybe because of the playoffs?

After I let Gigi out, I ask if he wants a glass of champagne.

"Yeah, that'd be perfect," he says quickly. I head

into the kitchen, pop open a bottle and pour two flutes. When I return to the living room, he's sitting on the couch next to my pup who's wearing a red and white bow tie.

It's the most darling thing I've ever seen. But my brow knits. "Did you get Gigi a Christmas bow tie?"

"She looks good, doesn't she?" he asks. He still sounds the slightest bit nervous.

"She wears most things well." I sit down on the couch with the two of them, and hand him a glass.

He takes a drink. I do too. In tandem, we set down our glasses.

He exhales sharply.

I've never seen him like this.

"Gabe, is everything okay?" I ask, right as he scoops up Gigi and sets her in my lap.

In no time, he drops down to one knee. I gasp.

"The bow tie's for both of you." He doesn't sound nervous anymore. He sounds intensely serious.

My heart climbs into my throat. "Oh my god," I whisper.

"I love you, Ellie Snow. I can't imagine a life without you. And all I want is to make you mine for the rest of my life. You're everything I've ever wanted, and I want to ask if you'll have me for the rest of your life. Will you marry me?"

As tears stream down my cheeks, I nod more times than I can count. "I can't wait to marry you."

He tugs on the dog's bow tie and a gorgeous diamond spills into his hand. There was a ring tucked into the bow tie. That's so Gabe, proposing with my dog's help.

"It's beautiful," I say reverently.

He slides it onto my finger and I am overwhelmed. By this life, this love, this man. I kiss him fiercely, declaring my yes.

We marry that summer, then honeymoon in Italy and Greece, where we indulge in delicious meals and fantastic scenarios—like when we pretend I booked the wrong place and he's the traveler who discovers me in his bed.

Then punishes me in delicious ways.

We return to Los Angeles after the most indulgent two weeks.

Soon though, it's time for training camp, so I wish him well as he heads to San Diego. He's going as a coach. He's working with the new receivers on the Mercenaries, and it's a perfect job for him.

I miss him the whole time, but I'm busy with my show.

When he comes home a few weeks later, we don't have to pretend we're the husband and wife who missed each other terribly. Because we are that couple. He scoops me up, carries me to the bedroom and then fucks the hell out of me.

Just what I want my husband to do.

* * *

A few years later on his birthday, I surprise him with a gift.

A pregnancy stick with two pink lines. His eyes flood with wonder and delight. "We're going to have a baby," he says. Then, with all the love I know he already feels, he drops to his knees and kisses my belly. I run my fingers through his hair. "Yes we are."

Then he rises, wraps his arms around me and kisses me tenderly. "You're going to be such a great mom."

"And you are going to be a terrific dad."

Some things you just know with your whole entire heart.

* * *

Do you want more from these characters right now? Keep reading for an extended epilogue! And you can grab Veronica's romance, Hazel's romance, and Brooke's romance now for FREE IN KU!

THE VIRGIN NEXT DOOR: Milo and Veronica

TWO A DAY: Drew and Brooke
MY SO-CALLED SEX LIFE: Hazel and Axel

You might also love The Ballers and Babes series of football romances and they're also **FREE in KU**! Turn the page for an excerpt!

EXCERPT - MOST VALUABLE PLAYBOY

Cooper

Always a bridesmaid.

No Action Armstrong.

Ball Cap Boy.

Mr. Clean.

The Unused Insurance Plan.

Oh wait. Here's one more, a personal fave.

Best Butt in the NFL.

Those are just some of the nicknames I've been given in the last few years. They don't bug me. Not one bit. They've all been true, especially the last one. You should see my ass. You can bounce a quarter off my cheeks.

Here's the thing—when you spend the first three

years of your career warming the bench for the best player in the league, you can't get a chip on your shoulder. You have to stay sharp and be ready for that moment when you swap out a ball cap for a helmet and get your pants dirty.

My time has finally come this season, and so far, we're winning.

But tonight isn't about what happens between the opening kickoff and the end of the fourth quarter.

Tonight is about the one game I've always dominated.

For the last few years, I've been the highest ticket item in the players' annual charity auction, and I can't help enjoying that. Because the guy I've backed up has been called a lot of things—a legend, the greatest ever, a titan of the game—but the one I most enjoy is "second-best-looking quarterback on the Renegades."

Hey, I didn't give him that name. The media did, deciding the dude who played second-string—me— had a prettier face. Before this season, I'd seen a grand total of 120 minutes of playing time in my first three years, but I've taken home the top honors in the charity auction, where some of the loveliest ladies come to bid on the players they want to take out for a night on the town.

Ah, the memories of those dates have warmed

my heart, and other parts, on the sidelines when the games were dull. Evenings in limos, testing the strength of the leather backseat, nights in hotels that lasted way past dawn, mutually and blissfully ignoring the *no physical contact between the winner and the player* rule.

Yeah, I've enjoyed the fuck out of being paraded on stage in front of hundreds of women, their slender arms lifted in the air, raising their bids higher on me than all the other guys. It's been my one chance to shine, even to stand out.

Those days are behind me, though, now that I'm finally leading the team down the field every single Sunday. I still expect to rake in top dollar for the charity I gladly support, but this time, I won't be living it up and letting loose after hours. I have a reputation to protect, and a season on the line.

Guess that means it's time to call an audible on the line of scrimmage.

Keep reading: Most Valuable Playboy!

Get your Gabe and Ellie extended epilogue by clicking here!

BE A LOVELY

Want to be the first to know of sales, new releases, special deals and giveaways? Sign up for my newsletter today!

Want to be part of a fun, feel-good place to talk about books and romance, and get sneak peeks of covers and advance copies of my books? Be a Lovely!

MORE BOOKS BY LAUREN

I've written more than 100 books! **All of these titles below are FREE in Kindle Unlimited!**

Double Pucked

A sexy, outrageous MFM hockey romantic comedy!

Puck Yes

A fake marriage, spicy MFM hockey rom com!

Thoroughly Pucked!

A brother's best friends +runaway bride, spicy MFM hockey rom com!

The Virgin Society Series

Meet the Virgin Society – great friends who'd do anything for each other. Indulge in these forbidden, emotionally-charged, and wildly sexy age-gap romances!

The RSVP

The Tryst

The Tease

The Dating Games Series

A fun, sexy romantic comedy series about friends in the city and their dating mishaps!

The Virgin Next Door

Two A Day

The Good Guy Challenge

How To Date Series (New and ongoing)

Friends who are like family. Chances to learn how to date again. Standalone romantic comedies full of love, sex and meet-cute shenanigans.

My So-Called Sex Life

Plays Well With Others

The Almost Romantic

Juliet's And Monroe's Romance (coming in June 2024)

Sawyer's Romance with Mystery Woman (August 2024)

Wilder's and Fable's Romance (November 2024)

Boyfriend Material

Four fabulous heroines. Four outrageous proposals. Four chances at love in this sexy rom-com series!

Asking For a Friend

Sex and Other Shiny Objects

One Night Stand-In

Overnight Service

Big Rock Series

My #1 New York Times Bestselling sexy as sin, irreverent,

male-POV romantic comedy!

Big Rock

Mister O

Well Hung

Full Package

Joy Ride

Hard Wood

Happy Endings Series

Romance starts with a bang in this series of standalones
following a group of friends seeking and avoiding love!

Come Again

Shut Up and Kiss Me

Kismet

My Single-Versary

Ballers And Babes

Sexy sports romance standalones guaranteed to make
you hot!

Most Valuable Playboy

Most Likely to Score

A Wild Card Kiss

Rules of Love Series

Athlete, virgins and weddings!

The Virgin Rule Book

The Virgin Game Plan

The Virgin Replay

The Virgin Scorecard

The Extravagant Series

Bodyguards, billionaires and hoteliers in this sexy, high-stakes series of standalones!

One Night Only

One Exquisite Touch

My One-Week Husband

The Guys Who Got Away Series

Friends in New York City and California fall in love in this fun and hot rom-com series!

Birthday Suit

Dear Sexy Ex-Boyfriend

The What If Guy

Thanks for Last Night

The Dream Guy Next Door

Always Satisfied Series

A group of friends in New York City find love and laughter in this series of sexy standalones!

Satisfaction Guaranteed

Never Have I Ever

Instant Gratification

PS It's Always Been You

The Gift Series

An after dark series of standalones! Explore your fantasies!

The Engagement Gift

The Virgin Gift

The Decadent Gift

The Heartbreakers Series

Three brothers. Three rockers. Three standalone sexy romantic comedies.

Once Upon a Real Good Time

Once Upon a Sure Thing

Once Upon a Wild Fling

Sinful Men

A high-stakes, high-octane, sexy-as-sin romantic suspense series!

My Sinful Nights

My Sinful Desire

My Sinful Longing

My Sinful Love

My Sinful Temptation

From Paris With Love

Swoony, sweeping romances set in Paris!

Wanderlust

Part-Time Lover

One Love Series

A group of friends in New York falls in love one by one in
this sexy rom-com series!

The Sexy One

The Hot One

The Knocked Up Plan

Come As You Are

Lucky In Love Series

A small town romance full of heat and blue collar heroes
and sexy heroines!

Best Laid Plans

The Feel Good Factor

Nobody Does It Better

Unzipped

No Regrets

An angsty, sexy, emotional, new adult trilogy about one
young couple fighting to break free of their pasts!

The Start of Us

The Thrill of It

Every Second With You

The Caught Up in Love Series

A group of friends finds love!

The Pretending Plot

The Dating Proposal

The Second Chance Plan

The Private Rehearsal

Seductive Nights Series

A high heat series full of danger and spice!

Night After Night

After This Night

One More Night

A Wildly Seductive Night

Joy Delivered Duet

A high-heat, wickedly sexy series of standalones that will set your sheets on fire!

Nights With Him

Forbidden Nights

Unbreak My Heart

A standalone second chance emotional roller coaster of a

romance

The Muse

A magical realism romance set in Paris

Good Love Series of sexy rom-coms co-written with Lili Valente!

I also write MM romance under the name L. Blakely!

Hopelessly Bromantic Duet (MM)

Roomies to lovers to enemies to fake boyfriends

Hopelessly Bromantic

Here Comes My Man

Men of Summer Series (MM)

Two baseball players on the same team fall in love in a forbidden romance spanning five epic years

Scoring With Him

Winning With Him

All In With Him

MM Standalone Novels

A Guy Walks Into My Bar

The Bromance Zone

One Time Only

The Best Men (Co-written with Sarina Bowen)

Winner Takes All Series (MM)

A series of emotionally-charged and irresistibly sexy standalone MM sports romances!

The Boyfriend Comeback

Turn Me On

A Very Filthy Game

Limited Edition Husband

Manhandled

If you want a personalized recommendation, email me at laurenblakelybooks@gmail.com!

CONTACT

I love hearing from readers! You can find me on Twitter at LaurenBlakely3, Instagram at LaurenBlakelyBooks, Facebook at LaurenBlakelyBooks, or online at LaurenBlakely.com. You can also email me at laurenblakelybooks@gmail.com